The Lane

The Lane

A Young Woman's Tale in the Heart of Dublin

Maura Rooney Hitzenbühler

Boston

First published by GemmaMedia in 2011.

GemmaMedia
230 Commercial Street
Boston, MA 02109 USA
www.gemmamedia.com

Printed in the United States of America

15 14 13 12 11   1 2 3 4 5

978-1-934848-40-1

Library of Congress Cataloging-in-Publication Data

Hitzenbühler, Maura Rooney
The lane : a young woman's tale in the heart of Dublin / Maura Rooney Hitzenbühler.
p. cm.
ISBN 978-1-934848-40-1
1. Unmarried mothers—Fiction. 2. Single parents—Fiction. 3. Young women—Ireland—Fiction. 4. Dublin (Ireland)—Social conditions—Fiction. I. Title.
PS3608.I89L36 2011
813'.6—dc22

2010049841

For

Maura Hitzenbühler Sargent

Maeve

Tara

William

and

Sean Patrick Hitzenbühler

CHAPTER 1

On a cool Friday in early spring, Kate, a tall and slender young woman carrying a suitcase stood at the entrance to the lane. The sign on a garden wall indicated "Redmond's Cottages." Francis had not mentioned that; he had merely called it The Lane. Perhaps, she thought, she had come to the wrong place. Finding no one to question, she walked slowly up the lane until she reached the water tap, the sole source of water for the people living in the lane.

As she turned left, the lane widened, and there before her were two rows of tiny cottages facing each other, separated by twenty feet of cobblestone courtyard, without steps or footpaths. In this deserted village within a village she stood where everything was clean, orderly, and without a soul present.

He does not seem like a man who would live in a place like this, she thought. He had said the fourth cottage on the right, she remembered as she walked past the neat, no-frills homesteads: no names, no door numbers, no bells. Nothing was displayed on these plain, brightly colored doors with the exception of brass keyholes and letterbox openings. As she reached the fourth cottage, she rapped on the tomato-red, painted door. He opened it, and as he stood there, she realized he would have to bend his head to enter or leave the cottage.

"You came!" he said in his usual soft voice.

"Did you think I wouldn't? Would you rather I hadn't?"

"No, no, not at all. Come in," he said as though saying, "you're here now, you might as well come in," she thought, as she hesitated at the threshold.

"I'll make us some tea." As he put the kettle on, he turned around and saw her gaze span the contents of the cottage. *Not much to offer a classy woman like her or any woman,* he deemed, as he too looked at the room he had not until this moment given much thought.

"Here, sit down," he urged, as he pulled out one of the three chairs at the small square table. There were no other chairs in the room save for the rocking chair by the fireplace. "The tea will be ready in a few minutes." She closed the door behind her and sat. He sat down opposite her.

"It's so quiet and peaceful here; it appears as though the cottages are unoccupied."

"Far from unoccupied," he told her. "There's never been a cottage vacant in my lifetime. Over the years, many of the cottages have been handed down to family members. All the cottages have but two rooms, a bedroom and an all-purpose room. Older people, for the most part, live here, although there are just two rather large families now. It's hard to imagine how they manage in two small rooms. It's assumed, though nobody would be so indelicate as to ask, that the male members of these families sleep in the bedroom, and mother and daughter sleep in the all-purpose room."

"Did you grow up here?"

"Yes, in this same cottage."

"Without house numbers, how does the mailman know which house to drop off the mail?"

"He knows that the even numbers are to the right, odd numbers on the left. We're the fourth house, so we're number eight."

This is a world unto itself. A world from another century, thought Kate.

He hesitated before speaking. "I brought in a pail of water. No indoor plumbing. You've passed the tap. There are six toilets and three shower stalls at the far end of the lane for all fourteen families." Hearing the kettle boil, he got up and prepared the tea. As he did so, he added, with a wave of his hand, "The bedroom's in there. There's a small yard in back." With his back towards her, he asked, "Did they verify it?"

"Verify it? Do you mean my pregnancy?"

"Yes."

She nodded. Then noticing he still had his back towards her, answered, "Yes."

"No doubt, then?" he asked turning towards her.

"None."

"There should be some bread in the bread box behind you. Would you give a look?"

"Yes," she answered as she opened the box and touched the half loaf of stale bread.

"Good. There's a chunk of cheese on the sideboard with the butter, milk and sugar. You'll find a knife in the drawer beneath it."

Opening the drawer, she found an assortment of hardware: a pen knife, some nails, a spanner, a screwdriver, some razor blades, a few spoons, three forks with bent prongs, a large bread knife, three dinner knives, a bottle opener, and some unidentifiable objects.

"I'm not much at keeping things in order. My mother, Lord rest her soul, kept everything shipshape. Now with the parents gone,

I tend to let things go. However, you can fix things whatever way you wish."

As he poured the tea into two mugs, she brought the bread, knife, cheese, milk, sugar and spoons to the table. In cutting the bread she asked, "Do you have regrets?"

"Ah no, it just took me by surprise. Is the tea to your liking?"

She nodded, and pondered her predicament. Why did she let herself get into this kind of situation? She could not tell her mother of her pregnancy, she was sure of that, and not at all sure of what life would hold for her from here onwards.

The tears seemed determined to fall, and she was equally determined to prevent them from doing so.

Think of something else, she told herself as they sat in silence.

She ate some stale bread with some cheese because she hadn't eaten all day and was hungry. She would go out tomorrow and buy some food. Would he offer her money to pay for it? Was there but one bed in the bedroom? Would they share the same bed? Her suitcase stood where she left it on coming into the cottage.

"Where can I hang my clothes?"

"There are hooks on the back of the door there and on the inside of the bedroom door."

"No closet! Do you have any spare clothes hangers?"

"Just take my shirts off and put them all on one hanger, and you can use the others."

He's easy to get along with, she thought. *Will that change in the months ahead when my womb expands? He's a very gentle soul. The baby could do a lot worse than have a man such as Francis for a father.* Breaking into her thoughts, she heard him speak.

"I'll be going out in a few minutes. There's a radio you might like to listen to, and I'll bring the newspaper on my return."

"Thank you."

Now the tears could fall, and they did, and going to the suitcase, she fumbled for a hankie, her body heaving with sobs. Physically and emotionally exhausted, she sought a place to lie down. Opening the bedroom door, she saw a large poorly-made bed with a blanket thrown across crumpled sheets. Unwashed clothing lay piled up in a corner, most likely gathered up from around the floor in an effort to tidy up the room. She was about to lie down on the bed and then remembered he had not offered her the bedroom. She pulled a sweater from her suitcase and wrapping herself in it, sank down into the rocking chair and fell asleep.

Upon awakening, she could not immediately recollect where she was. As she scanned the darkened room, she remembered: Francis' cottage! Looking at her watch, she realized it was half past five in the morning. Although it would pain her to do so, she knew she could sell the watch her beloved father had given her. It would have to be under dire circumstances, though. She lovingly touched the band of the watch.

Suddenly she heard a rustling noise. Mice! No, just Francis.

"You were asleep when I got in yesterday evening, so I moved softly not to waken you. Would you like some tea? It's already made," he said.

"Yes, I'll get it."

"You can sleep in the bed. I've straightened it out a bit. I should be at my uncle's farm by six. I'll be back before five this evening."

"Thanks." *What does he expect?* she wondered. *I slept with him once before. I'm carrying this child, and I'm settling down in his house.*

Rising from the rocking chair, she shivered, and passing in front of him, poured tea into a mug. She took the tea into the bedroom and closed the door behind her, and then wondered if she should have done that. She heard her mother's often-repeated words 'Don't bite the hand that feeds you.' Discovering there was no lock on the door, her worry that it might appear that she was shutting him out was for naught.

Awakening later in the morning, alone and feeling sick, she felt she had to vomit. She hastened to the other room, and grabbing her raincoat from the hook on the door, opened the door and ran swiftly and barefooted up to the toilets, her coat flung around her shoulders and her hand across her mouth. Kneeling beside the toilet she vomited. Cold and exhausted, she sat on the concrete floor and leaned against the wooden partition until she was sure she was finished. She had been sitting there, growing more numb by the moment, when she felt drops of rain on her neck. Struggling to her feet, she reached up and pulled the chain. She walked back down the lane, past the cottage and washed her hands by the water tap. Then cupping her hands, she filled them with water and rinsed out the bad taste from her mouth. There was no need to hurry out of the rain, even if she had had the energy to do so, for she was soaked from her hair to her cold bare feet.

After she entered the cottage, she immediately put on a full kettle from the water that Francis had brought in before he left.

As it warmed, she fetched some soap and a towel and placed a large hand-basin on the floor. Stripping, she stepped into the basin and carefully poured the warm water over her head, and it flowed downward into the basin as she washed. Then using more water, she rinsed off. She dried herself and dressed. With the remaining water she made tea and drank it, her hands around the hot cup and her feet securely tucked beneath her in the rocking chair. With a second cup of tea she ate the remaining crust of bread from yesterday without butter in order to appease her queasy stomach.

She was thankful that Francis had not witnessed this episode. She did not want to think of food, but she knew she needed to feed the baby growing within her. She must engage Francis in conversation so that each of then could know what to expect from the other. Would he bring up marriage? Did he plan to marry her? Did she want to marry him? She had connected with him to legitimize the baby. Yes, there were many things they needed to talk about, but the most immediate was the need for food. She could make dinner for them if she had some ingredients to do so. Her mother's cook, the soul of patience, had taught her to cook.

'Mother!' she thought. Since her father's death her mother had lived alone in her house with three large bedrooms, two permanently empty. She could have moved back home if her father were there to buffer her against her mother's wrath. No matter how badly Francis might treat her, it would be like soft falling rain compared to what her mother would shower upon her if she were to return home pregnant or with a child and no husband. The scandal, as her mother would see it, would be too much to bear.

Brothers, Kieran and Rory, twelve and thirteen years older than Kate, their mother's 'fair haired' boys, made her proud. One had followed in their father's footsteps by becoming a dentist, while the other had become a college professor. Each had married. Kieran and his wife had given their mother two granddaughters, all in the proper order. Rory and Gwen were without children.

Yes, she had been a disappointment to her mother. Why compound that by adding more grief and shame to the family name by returning home? Be that as it may, she would now have to concentrate on how to get someone as nonverbal as Francis to talk.

She would not have access to the money her father had left her until she was twenty-five years old. Right now she was three months less than twenty-two and just out of nursing school. She was fortunate to get a position in the hospital right out of school. And yet, in the six months she had been working she had saved very little. There was the rent for the shared flat, transportation and food expenses, and the clothing sprees her friends and she had gone on together. What need would she have now of three-inch high heels, cashmere sweaters, and fancy dresses? What she regretted most was the money spent with her nursing friends at restaurants and pubs when off duty. It had been their first taste of freedom after strict boarding schools and then regimented nurses training. Now she was hiding out from her friends lest the news of her pregnancy travel to her home town and to her family.

She would, from necessity, need to be frugal. In a very short time, food cost could eat away her savings leaving her without money for a carriage or crib or other baby needs. As soon as her pregnancy showed, she knew she would be out of a job. The hospital's strict rules had to be obeyed. No shortage of nurses in Ireland, and more than enough here to supply hospitals in England and elsewhere.

Kate was still curled up in the rocking chair when Francis entered. Looking at her watch she realized it was close to noon.

"I just work to eleven on Saturdays. Did I not mention that?" he responded to her surprised expression.

"I would have prepared dinner but there's no food in the cottage," she told him.

"Aw, yes. I eat at the farm. I told my aunt I wouldn't be having the midday meal with them, as you were new to the place and I thought I'd come back and see if you needed anything. Would you like to go out and eat?"

"Yes, that would be nice."

"Get your coat so, and we'll be off."

Oh, Lord, grant me patience, she thought. *I've told him I would have made dinner if there were food in the house, and he offers this temporary solution. Keep trying.*

"I'm afraid I've eaten the last of the bread from the breadbox," she told him while putting on her coat.

"Not to worry, Kate, the shops are only about a mile away."

How extraordinarily dense! she thinks. *I can find shops. It is money I need! Don't upset the apple cart. He has no obligation to me. If he hadn't offered his cottage, even in the off-hand manner in which he did, I'd have nowhere to go but back home. His meals are taken care of by his aunt. I'm on my own. How long will it be before I show and am forced to resign? How long will my savings hold out? How much does a baby's crib and a carriage cost?* Kate pondered, and in finding no answers, put it all aside.

"Does your uncle need you at the farm on Sunday?"

"No."

He goes to bed around nine o'clock and rises at five o'clock. That would eliminate an evening film, she reasoned.

"Perhaps we could go the cinema on Sunday afternoon?"

"Yes," he answered, noticeably pleased at the suggestion. "Is there one particular film you'd like to see?"

"We could look in the paper when we get home to see what's being shown."

She had said 'home' without thinking. Had he noticed?

On Saturday they chose a film to see the following afternoon. Settling down for the evening, a peaceful contentment settled upon them as he shared his newspaper with her until the Irish News on RTÉ radio. Afterwards they listened to some Irish music programs, then the news on the BBC.

He made no demands on her, and he did not enter the bedroom when she was there. But this was Saturday night, it was almost eleven o'clock, and neither of them seemed to know what to do about the sleeping accommodations. At midnight when they were having difficulty fighting off sleep, she in the rocking chair and he on the hard, uncomfortable kitchen chair, she ventured to ask, if he wished to share the bed with her. It was, no doubt, on both of their minds, but Francis seemed stunned by the question.

"No, Kate, I wouldn't want to do anything that might hurt the baby. You take the bed."

This statement moved her, and there arose in her an urge to kiss him, but she refrained from doing so. She marveled at the fact that Francis, who worked with farm animals, could be so unfamiliar with a woman's body.

"The baby is quite safe within me."

"What if I were to roll over onto it during the night?"

"I'd automatically move away."

He smiled at her confidence and his own insecurity on such matters.

"Well, you're a nurse. You would know such things."

"Good night," she said as she walked into the bedroom. About a half hour later, he stood at the door.

"If you're sure it will be all right, I'd like to get into bed."

"I'm sure."

What were Francis's intentions? she wondered. He merely lay beside her in the darkened room. Would that continue? If more were to happen would she want it to? Even that she was unsure of. Yet, she liked knowing he was there beside her. Waking during the night, she felt the heat of his body next to hers, and moving closer to him, she fell back into sleep.

Sunday morning found her bolting out the front door and racing up the yard to the toilets. As her stomach emptied, she was concerned by the length of time she was spending away from the cottage, and didn't want to worry Francis; but she could not run the risk of leaving too early and having to suffer the embarrassment of having to make more trips back and forth. It was better that she stay put, she decided, and wished she had had time to put a heavy sweater on under her raincoat.

"What happened? Are you all right? Is the baby all right?" Francis asked with great concern as she entered the cottage.

"I'm fine. The baby is, too. It's called morning sickness. It will pass."

"When?"

"It's difficult to say. A few weeks! It's nothing to worry about."

"You look so pale. Sit down. I'll make you some tea. Is there anything I can get you?"

"I need something light to eat."

"What would you like? I'll go to the paper shop. They're open on Sunday, and they sell a few food items."

"That would be lovely. Some bread and cream crackers or any kind of crackers they might have."

Francis hurried out to the paper store as though her time to deliver had come.

Later that day, after the movie, he invited her to a pub. When she explained that she would not drink while carrying the child, he chose a pub wherein they could have tea and a very good meal. That night she put the crackers on the small table by the bed, explaining as she did so that eating crackers before rising might keep the morning sickness at bay.

After leaving work on Monday, Kate spent almost twenty pounds on food, which she hoped to stretch out with good management. Since Francis ate his meals at the farm, she hoped to be able to take care of her needs. She was fast growing very attached to Francis, and whenever he felt comfortable with it, she would welcome his more intimate presence in the bed. She sensed he liked her, nay, might even love her. She now looked forward with more optimism to the baby's birth and felt fortunate that this child would have such a good man as a father. Kate eagerly awaited Francis's homecoming each day, and he was always happy to see her. Life in the cottage continued in a pleasant, comfortable manner.

Outside the cottage, however, she was not fully accepted. The men from the lane, on seeing Francis, stopped and discussed the soccer game, politics, or shared a joke or two with him, and the women approached Francis fondly, greeting him as one of their own as they stopped and chatted with him. All Kate ever received was a smile and a 'good morning' or 'evening' from the women and a tip of the cap from the men. None of them stopped to speak with her. She was an outsider in this very tight-knit village.

"Do you want to get married?" Francis asked one evening, about six weeks later, as they stood up to retire for the night. Taken by surprise that what she had been wondering about was now actually happening, Kate was without words.

"I believe you were willing to come here solely for the baby's sake. I know you are used to much better than this," he told her, indicating their surroundings. Before he could continue, she cut him off.

"Yes. Yes, I will marry you."

His broad smile was reassuring.

"When you walked in that first day, I could hardly believe my good fortune. For weeks, I feared that arriving home one day I might find you had left. The time we've been together in this cottage has been for me the happiest of times, and I believe you are content here."

He had not mentioned he loved her, but she knew that was what he meant, and it was as close as he could get to saying what he wished to convey.

"More than content, Francis. Happy, very happy."

"Then we'll do it," and picking up the candle, he put his arm around her, as they walked into the bedroom.

CHAPTER 2

"It will be a small wedding, will it not?" Kate asked as they divided the newspaper the following evening.

"Whatever you want it to be, it will be. There'll only be my uncle and aunt on my side."

"Nobody from the lane invited?"

"It might be a bit confusing to these good people, Kate, to be inviting them to a wedding when they are assuming we're already married."

"Oh, yes. I'll invite my cousin, Sheila, as my maid-of-honor."

"Not your parents? You do have family, do you not?"

"Yes, my mother, two brothers and their wives, and my older brother's two children, an uncle, two aunts, my grandfather, and some cousins. Since they don't know I'm pregnant, I'd rather let them know after the fact—perhaps in a year or two."

"Your mother would not approve of me?"

"She would not approve of the order in which I have proceeded. She would be horrified to find me pregnant, and my brothers, especially my younger brother, would have difficulty accepting my condition."

"I've got to get you married fast," Francis said with a devilish smile. "We could get married in the church I attend on Sundays with my uncle and aunt, and afterwards we could all go to the nearby hotel for lunch, if you wish."

"That sounds wonderful."

"Incidentally, where did you get that wedding band you've been wearing?"

"In Woolworth's. Fake gold for a faked marriage! I could not be pregnant without a wedding band on my finger!"

"Meet me at the Pillar House on Saturday after work, and I'll buy you a wedding band."

"I'll be there."

"Perhaps we can take a ride out and visit the priest next Sunday to get things rolling."

"Yes." After a moment's hesitation, Kate asked, "What have you told your aunt and uncle about us?"

"Well, they know you're pregnant and living here with me at the cottage. I believe they'll be very happy to hear we're going to get married regardless of what order we are doing it. 'I'll be a grand-aunt!' said my aunt, who was very excited when I told her about the baby. Their only child died at birth, and she and Ned were never able to have another child. You'll be able to meet them next Sunday when we go out to Swords to discuss our wedding with the priest."

Francis and Kate attended mass in the church where they would be married, and the priest accepted Mary and Ned's invitation, extended earlier in the week, to have dinner with them to discuss the wedding plans. Mary and Ned were two of the kindest people Kate had ever met. She felt completely at home with them and very happy that they would be part of her baby's life. A moment of sadness clouded this happy occasion when she thought, if only, like Francis, she too, could tell her family about the baby. She could have told her father. He would have been disappointed but he would have stood by her, she believed, and have accepted the baby as his grandchild.

After she bought some groceries in the shops, Kate noticed the bright green telephone booth, like a beacon in a storm, a block away. She rushed toward it as fast as she could while she struggled with the bag of groceries and a floor mop.

Putting down everything she was carrying, she took out the coins she had received in change. She put one in the phone slot and dialed her cousin Sheila's home. More coins! She dropped them in. She heard the phone ring on the other end and anxiously waited. It was not Sheila's voice but Sheila's mother's voice she heard. It could not be! Yet it was. Aunt Jenny, who shunned the telephone, had picked up the receiver.

"Hello, I can't hear you."

Just in time, she stopped herself before exclaiming, 'Aunt Jenny.'

"Hello. May I speak with Sheila?"

"She isn't here now," she answered and continued slowly from a prepared message. "Tell me your name and telephone number, and I'll give it to her when she gets back."

Aunt Jenny did not recognize her voice on the phone. Back from where? What name could she give that Sheila would be able to decipher.

"Back from where?"

"From her holidays, of course. She left last night for Malta. She'll be there for a fortnight and then will spend two days in London and be back on a Wednesday."

That's cutting it close, Kate thought. Sheila won't be back until the Wednesday before the wedding.

"Please tell Sheila it is her friend who attended 'The Taming of the Shrew' with her." Her aunt laboriously wrote down and repeated each word, while Kate kept dropping coins in the slot. She was about to thank her when her aunt spoke as though reading aloud.

"I must ask you for your telephone number?"

"I don't have a telephone."

"You're speaking on the telephone."

"Yes, but it is not my telephone."

"Should you be using someone else's telephone?" her aunt reprimanded.

"I'm using a coin-operated telephone. I'm phoning from one of the green boxes." Her aunt was confused but now she understood.

Jenny, an unstoppable talker when face to face with a person, but not comfortable with a telephone, did not reply. Kate said goodbye and hung up.

On the day Sheila was expected back, Kate telephoned again and once more Sheila's mother answered. Asking to speak with Sheila, a sad voice related that Sheila's grandfather had died during the night. When she inquired further, Kate learned that her grandfather would be waked from Wednesday through Friday evening. On Saturday morning the funeral mass would be held followed by his burial.

Kate was shocked to learn of her grandfather's death and stunned by the realization that his burial would take place on her wedding day. Though not superstitious, Kate had the haunting feeling it was a bad omen. She did not ask if her previous telephone call had been made known to Sheila. Sheila would not be at her wedding.

"Don't go giving that shirt of mine any notions," Francis said, as he watched Kate iron his only dress shirt later that evening. "It might expect to be ironed again the next time it's washed."

"Heavens forbid it should have such expectations," Kate laughed.

"I'll take it with me. When the chores are completed and I've cleaned up, I'll put it on and look respectable for you."

Kate brushed Francis's blazer and wondered in what distant year it had been purchased.

"We must leave here at five o'clock tomorrow morning."

"Five?" Kate questioned. "The wedding isn't until eleven o'clock!"

"Yes, but there are cows to milk and chores that must be done."

"Then I'd better get myself to bed to be able to get up at four in the morning," and taking the iron from the fire grate, she put it in the yard to cool off before going to bed.

In her fantasies as a young girl, she had never envisioned rising at four o'clock in the morning on her wedding day while her husband-to-be whistled a merry tune. No wedding gown! No friends gathering for a bridal tea! No family present for this happy occasion! She would wear one of the dresses she had purchased in that other life as a newly graduated nurse where she and her friends in carefree exuberance went shopping. Can a body be both happy and sad, she asked herself, happy to be marrying Francis, and sad that her family would not be sharing this very special occasion with her? Francis brought a cup of tea to her in bed and scattered her thoughts.

"Are you happy, Kate?"

"Yes, very happy."

"No doubts?"

"None."

Climbing into the bed, he encircled her in his arms and kissed her. "I'd like to stay in bed with you all day."

"There are cows to be milked and chores to be done," Kate mimicked.

"And a wedding ceremony to be performed," Francis smiled, as he stood up. "We must leave in fifteen minutes."

"I haven't showered."

"You can do that at the farm."

"No breakfast?"

"No time."

After hanging his shirt, trousers, blazer and Kate's dress in the van, Francis waited while Kate hastily dressed and then stepped into the van. He suggested she get some sleep while he drove. She closed her eyes but sleep was out of the question.

Ned had already started the chores when they arrived. Francis stepped from the van and joined Ned while Kate and Mary went into the house, bringing the clothes with them. Mary prepared a hot bath for Kate from the water in the rain barrel into which Mary had placed a small mesh bag of aromatic herbs from her garden. The tub stood in a screened off section of the kitchen and the aroma of Mary's baking, mixed with the scent of herbs, filled the spacious kitchen. This was her first precious luxury since she met Francis, and it relaxed every bone and fiber of her body as she soaked in its warmth and fragrance, transporting her beyond time and space. Heavenly!

Kate was sitting in the sun drying her hair when Ned came back to the house. From the kitchen door, Mary called out, "Where is Francis?"

"He finished up before me and left."

"Well, since you're here first, go ahead and bathe, so that the tub will be free when Francis gets here."

About twenty minutes later, Francis returned carrying a bunch of wild flowers and green ferns.

"How beautiful," Mary declared, as Francis handed Kate the flowers.

"Yes, absolutely beautiful," Kate confirmed, as she flung her arms around her fiancé and kissed him.

"We must tie them up with ribbons. Come, Kate, and pick some ribbons from my basket."

Since there were purple, blue and pale yellow flowers in the bunch, Kate chose a blue, a purple and a buttercup yellow ribbon and entwined them around the flowers and ferns, making the loveliest of bouquets.

Ned had cleaned and polished the old sidecar, and the women sat on each side as Francis and Ned rode up front and drove the horses.

The stone church where they were married had an aisle that was the length of two horses and carts, with wooden pews on each side and a small rail separating the sanctuary from the main body of the church. From the choir loft, the organist played as Francis and Ned came in by the side entrance close to the altar. Local people, neighbors, friends, and farmers and their wives rose when moments later, Kate and Mary entered the church.

One could have heard a match drop in the silence that befell the congregation when Francis and Kate professed their vows to each other before God and their fellowmen. As they walked down the aisle as husband and wife, Francis told Kate his parents were married in this church, as were Ned and Mary.

Back at the house, the neighbors arrived, as did a large soft package. Each woman brought her food specialty and placed it on the table. As the women uncovered plates, bowls and platters, Kate marveled at the large array of delicious foods. Soon everyone was eating, drinking, talking and laughing. When all had eaten, the women cleared the table while the fiddler tuned his violin. Then the package was placed on the table. Mary and Ned brought Kate and Francis forward as the people gathered around the table and waited for the newly wedded couple to open the parcel. Francis pulled the string off and Kate pulled back the paper to expose a most beautiful handmade quilt, a gift from Ned's and Mary's friends and neighbors. All eyes were on Kate to see her reaction. Her delight was in full bloom, and her gratitude at their kindness overwhelmed her. Mary explained that she and the women had met two nights a week, at each other's houses, to bring their finished pieces and sew them together. Then the women took over and told how they had decided on a design. They related their mishaps, the fun they had in this endeavor, and who among them made each particular part of the quilt.

"Some of us were left on those evenings to do the washing up after supper," Sean Coogan said, speaking for the men assembled.

"You got supper?" Mike Rafferty exclaimed to much laughter.

"Let's not waste this good music," one of the women spoke out bringing the joking to a close.

Ned and Mary obliged by being the first to dance, as encouragement to the others to do likewise. They received a round of applause. Then others joined in the dance.

Will Francis ask me to dance? Does Francis know how to dance? Kate wondered. Nobody would dance with her, she knew, until Francis had done so. Kate stood looking at Ned and Mary, two perfectly matched people, as they enjoyed the dance, and had difficulty keeping her feet from stepping to the music.

I must not look too anxious. I must wait.

Kate could see Francis receiving congratulations as he talked and laughed with the men. Some wives claimed their husbands who followed them to the dance floor. Old and young and ages in between danced. Suddenly Francis stood beside her. She had not heard him approach.

"May I have this dance?" he asked.

"You most certainly may," she answered. He led her onto the floor, the boards of which creaked under the feet of the dancers. As soon as Francis and Kate moved onto the dance floor, all other dancers immediately stopped and moved to the outer edges of the floor and stood in a circle.

She had never before danced with Francis. This was a new and exciting experience, being in his arms as they danced along to the fiddler's tune, oblivious to all around them. *How did a girl-shy man like Francis learn how to dance so well?* Kate did not want the music to stop.

After they danced together, they sat down. They were no sooner seated than the fiddler played music to set dancing, and Francis and Kate were gently pulled back to the dance floor. Joining hands with others, they danced forward and back, as they crisscrossed, changed partners, passed through those opposite them and danced from one end of the room to the other like the waves of the sea.

Happy and exhausted, Francis and Kate stayed overnight at the farm. After a hearty breakfast the next morning, they left for home laden with food from the previous day's feast. Francis surprised Kate with tickets for The Abbey Theatre, followed by dinner in the Grisham Hotel.

Francis and Kate returned to the lane as husband and wife.

Kate was in her seventh month of pregnancy when Francis came home one night later than usual and deeply troubled. While in the bank taking care of his uncle's business, Francis made a devastating discovery. He had overhead Harry Browne brag that he, a man about town and smooth-talking womanizer, had gotten Kate pregnant. Francis hastily left the bank for he could not bear to hear more.

Francis realized that Kate met him in The Mouse That Roared just a few nights after the supposed encounter with Browne. Within three weeks she had accepted Francis' offer to drive her to her flat after she had claimed she had missed the last bus. He spent the night there. Would she have spoken to him in the Mouse that night if she were not pregnant? Francis doubted it. *It wasn't me she wanted but a name for the child. Now that she had that, have I served my usefulness? Is all else that happened between us a lie?*

Francis remembered the day he opened his cottage door and found her standing there. He was afraid to reach out and touch her as though in doing so, he might find she was an illusion, a figment of his imagination. She could have made a better marriage under more acceptable circumstances. *Why Harry Browne? What attracted her to slime like Browne? Why could she not have told me the truth? I would have married her and accepted the child as my own. Yet she chose to deceive me, made a mockery of love and trust. Did she ever love me? Was there any truth in anything she said or was it all a lie?*

Francis didn't raise his voice, but Kate felt the depth of his anger in the low guttural sound that emerged from him and the look of hurt and betrayal in his eyes. True to his nature, he uttered the bare minimum of words necessary to convey to her what he had discovered.

Kate, on being confronted with this horror from the past, was without words. In her happiness with Francis, she had put her encounter with Harry Browne out of her mind in the hope that it would leave her life forever. She was devastated by this turn of events. She had never intended to hurt Francis. All she had wanted was to protect the child and give it a father. Everything had come together so beautifully only to split wide apart, like a dropped melon. She had not expected to fall in love with Francis, but she had been willing to be a good wife to him no matter what course life would take. On finding Francis loved her, too, she had felt heaven blessed.

As he packed a borrowed suitcase, she tried to tell him how sorry she was, explaining that her thoughts at that time had been for the child she carried. She revealed that in the time they had been together, she had fallen in love with him. Unfortunately, she was unable to convince him. After throwing some things into the case, he left the house; he did not say "goodbye."

For a moment she stood dazed, then collected herself and hurried down the lane after him, grabbing his arm to stop him, trying to persuade him to stay. But all she could do was to slow him down for a moment. He took two twenty-pound notes from his pocket and thrust them at her.

"Please don't leave," she begged. "I love you. I'm truly sorry. Can we discuss this?" She was now trotting beside him to keep pace with his large strides. Defeated she stopped, and in one last attempt called to him, "Will you return?" He did not answer, but continued down the lane not looking back even as he turned the corner.

For several moments, Kate stared at the space where Francis had been before he turned the corner and walked out of her life. Slowly she walked back to the cottage remembering the first time she walked up the lane and Francis had opened the cottage door and invited her in.

To her embarrassment she discovered, in the quiver of a curtain, that the lane people, who lived very private lives, had looked out from their windows at what had taken place. As she entered the cottage, she closed the door behind her, closing herself off from curious eyes. For three days, or was it four, or perhaps as many as five, she remained in the cottage, too disheartened to function.

Emerging from bed to go up the lane one night, she caught a glimpse of herself in Francis' shaving mirror. She was horrified by her appearance, unwashed face surrounded by tangled hair, still wearing the dress she had worn when pleading with Francis as he strode down the lane.

Suddenly, the realization that she had eaten nothing but tea and bread in three days and had felt no hunger set off an alarm within her. *Here I am,* she thought, *wallowing in self-pity and neglecting to eat properly while carrying my baby.* Francis' leaving had been a terrible blow.

She thought, *just as I fell in love with him, he left. I should have known that in a small place like this secrets fly on the wind and land on doorsteps. Our doorstep! Francis could have thrown me out of the cottage knowing this was Harry's child that I'm carrying. He would have had every right to do so, but he is too decent to do that. I did him a dreadful wrong. Ah Francis, how I wish I didn't make such a disaster of your life as well as mine.*

Pulling herself together, she wondered where she had put the money Francis had given her. After looking on the table, chairs, and underneath them without finding it, she brought the candle over to the fireplace and found the pound notes there on the floor by the rocking chair. Patting her stomach, she said aloud, "You need food to grow on." She went to bed that evening with something she thought had abandoned her, a small spark of hope.

After breakfast the following morning, Kate, with a towel on her arm, walked to the shower. It was hardly necessary to pull the water handle, for a steady rain began just as she had stepped into the stall. After soaping herself, she turned her face upwards to the falling rain. It flowed down upon her like a sacred stream from the heavens, cleansing her body and refreshing her soul.

Kate had many things to do before the baby arrived. She put a full kettle of water on to heat. Going into the yard, she took down the washtub from its nail in the shed and placed it on a bench. The rain had stopped, and the sun was now shining brightly in the sky. Gathering her clothing, the bed linens and towels and the shirts Francis had left behind, she brought them into the yard. Then, taking the kettle of hot water, she filled the washtub and proceeded to wash the clothes. She would wear Francis' shirts for the remainder of her pregnancy, since every piece of clothing she owned was too tight a fit. Should Francis not return by the time the baby was ready to enter school, she would cut down his shirts to make the child shirts or dresses.

At mid-morning with a full line of clothes hanging from the line, Kate refilled the kettle and put it on the flame. Then she removed all the clutter and knick knacks from the top of the bureau, sideboard, and shelves. Francis had said she could fix the place as she deemed fit, but she had not wanted to remove what she surmised to be his mother's treasures. Kate picked up a small Dutch boy in blue and white delft, an import from Holland. Examining it closer she found it had had an accident, for the head had been glued back onto the body. Did Francis play with it as a child?

From a small postage card photograph, an attractive young couple smiled out at Kate from over the years. It must have been taken while they were on their honeymoon; people in those days did not travel unless on their honeymoon or immigrating. In the left hand corner of the photograph, in faded, small, neat handwriting were the words "The Isle of Man" and a date. It was, she assumed, their first time off Irish soil. They went from one small island to a smaller island with much less to offer. A weekend on an island close by was an adventure for them. She believed from the family resemblance they must be Francis' parents. Since it was taken long before color photography, Kate could only wonder from which of his parents Francis inherited his red hair.

A baby photograph of Francis and one taken in his first Communion suit; one of Francis, at about eight years old, as he rode a horse on Ned and Mary's farm. All photographs stood in the same spot his mother had left them many years ago. On another shelf was a photograph of Francis as he stood between his parents and

Mary and Ned after being confirmed. One showed Francis fishing with his father and Ned. Behind an unused dusty china teapot was a family photograph taken at Christmastime at the farm with his parents and aunt and uncle. She would clean and display these photographs.

All but one religious statue she would pack in a cardboard box that she found in the bedroom, along with leprechauns; cups and saucers all stating where people had gone; good-luck charms; vases too small for any but a single small flower; decorated plates which were not meant to be eaten off; small hand-painted boxes; figurines received from people from various places in Ireland they had visited; and various other objects with no purpose other than to be displayed.

Cleaning off all surfaces and removing all the books from the shelves and floor of the bedroom, she stacked them on the bed to be sorted later. As the kettle came to a boil, Kate swept every nook and cranny of the house and then scrubbed the floors. It was past three o'clock by the time she finished. Leaving the back door to the yard open in order to dry the floors, she stood for a moment looking into the cottage, now with years of grime and neglect removed, and smiled. Yes, she believed, it was a quaint and loveable home. Tomorrow she would tackle the yard and the shed.

After supper, while she browsed through the pile of books, she selected Boris Pasternak's *Dr. Zhivago*. She read late into the night until the candle had burned down. Before falling asleep, her last conscious thoughts were of love and betrayal.

Standing in the yard the next morning she decided that it was not a fit place for a child to play, and set about cleaning out the shed. She removed old bicycle tubes; bald tires; glass jars caked with dirt; rusting nails, a hammer, a watering can; a kitchen chair with one leg missing; rusting pieces of metal; parts of something unknown; and an old mason hot-water bottle which she checked for soundness. Finding it did indeed have a leak; she discarded it into the pile of rubbish she planned to bring down the lane to the street below on the day the rubbish collectors made their rounds.

Discovering just a half-full bin of turf, which wouldn't last the winter, she threw the three-legged chair on top of the turf for firewood. Other than the turf, all that now remained in the shed was the hammer and the watering can.

Examining all the flowerpots scattered around the yard, she discarded all the broken ones. She washed all those in good condition and placed them in the shed.

When all the rubbish was removed, she swept and washed down the yard. Then she showered and prepared dinner.

As she started to cook, she noticed an envelope on the floor underneath the mail slot. She picked it up. It was addressed to Francis Egan and by its envelope she surmised it was some official notice or a bill. Should she bring it to him at the farm? She knew the location, but not the address. The mailman would, in all likelihood, deliver it if she readdressed it to "Egan's Farm, Swords." That might be risky if this were an important document, she realized, and so she opened the piece of mail. It was a rates bill. She hadn't thought about taxes! The tax on the cottage was more than the remaining balance in her bank account. Could Francis be expected to pay the taxes on the cottage in which he no longer lived? Was it now her liability?

The following day, Kate pondered the possibilities that might be available to her as she ironed. The aroma of the lamb and vegetables as they simmered on the stove filled the cottage. It was such a delicious and comforting smell; it made Kate temporarily forget about upcoming expenses. She had a choice of going to the Charity Ward to have the baby, or delivering it in the cottage. Being familiar with the Charity Ward and its unfortunate patients, she decided on the latter.

She would get in touch with her brother Kieran, the one family member, she believed, most likely to be sympathetic to her, but wondered how she could do that without revealing her dilemma. Perhaps she could tell him she wanted to enroll at University for another degree and needed money to live on. Could she draw on her inheritance for such a purpose?

Would another lie matter? Her whole life, from her meeting with Francis onwards, was a lie. That one lie gave birth to many lies. She had always thought of herself as an honest person. Then she got pregnant, and lies attached themselves to her like flies on flypaper.

She might be able to get a position as a night nurse when the baby was several months old, if she could hire someone in the lane to watch him during the night. That, however, was more than half a year away. How could she provide for the baby and herself in the interim?

After finishing the ironing, she stood the iron in the yard to cool off, and coming back into the cottage, she heard a knock on the door. No neighbors, actually nobody at all, had ever come knocking on her door during her stay in the cottage.

Don't get your hopes up. Francis isn't coming back, and if it were he at the door, he'd have no need to knock; he has a key. She would like to show him how nice the cottage looked. Would he care?

Opening the door, she was surprised and overjoyed to see her cousin standing there.

"Sheila!"

"This is a damn hard place to find," Sheila declared as she stepped into the cottage and embraced Kate. For a moment Kate could do nothing but smile in happiness and hold onto her cousin's embrace.

"Does this place reappear every hundred years?"

"Not that I know of," Kate laughed, and the sound of her laughter was like a long lost friend returning. "This is Ireland, not Scotland. How did you find me?"

"In trying to locate you, I heard from someone who knew Harry Browne, and he said you were one of Harry's ex-girlfriends. I explained that you were my cousin. He said you had picked up with Francis Egan, and although he didn't know where Egan lived, he knew he worked on a farm in Swords. Well, I found the Egan farm, introduced myself to his aunt, and waited in her kitchen until Francis had finished his chores. She is a sweet lady, who insisted on making tea and serving some of the most delicious homemade bread and cake imaginable. Egan certainly is the silent type, but otherwise quite pleasant and very handsome, I might add. He, of course, gave me directions, and here I am."

"You're so resourceful."

"The reason I'm here is because I'm running away."

"Sheila, do be serious," Kate pleaded through her laughter.

"Well, that's what my mother calls it. She said, in her day, nice girls didn't leave home until they married."

"Where are you going?"

"Just across the pond, but to my mother it might as well be Timbuktu."

"England," Kate gasped in horror. "It might as well be Australia, for I'll not be able to visit you."

"We'll keep in touch. I promise. My mother has told me in full the gory details of Jack the Ripper. She sees danger lurking in every street and lane in London. Mom's convinced England is filled with Ripper types. Mom asks, how can it be otherwise? Not only for those who were a part of the mayhem of fighting in the war, but for those huddled on the underground platforms, and in air raid shelters living in fear while bombs hailed down on them each night, and wondering if they'd get out alive or take a direct hit and be buried alive under the rubble. It was enough to drive them crazy, Mom said, and crazy they were."

"Might she be happier if you went to America?"

"Mom doesn't have a positive view of American men either. She remembers what the English soldiers said of the Americans in uniform during the war. 'They were oversexed, overpaid, and over here.'"

"Mom recalled," Sheila continued, "the tales that came from

America as told by English war brides. There was a soldier who said he was in the newspaper business, and his war bride found he sold newspapers from an stand by a subway station. And another who said he was in the dairy business who actually went from street to street selling ice cream. Then there were the horror stories of cultural difference, in-law problems, and homesickness. Of course, it was the most bizarre cases that made the headlines. Not much was told of those who settled down and were happy."

"I left a message with your mother, and I didn't know if you had deciphered it."

"Yes, indeed, after Mom finally remembered to give it to me! Grandfather's death was a terrible blow to her."

"Aunt Jenny didn't recognize my voice."

"I usually tell her ahead of time that I'll be phoning her at a certain time, and when I do, she'll ask, 'Is this Sheila?' Of course, she rarely answers the damn thing. Now tell me, how come you're living in Francis Egan's place?"

"It's a long horrible story. I'll put on the kettle, and then tell you the whole sorry mess, or would you like some stew?"

"Do you have enough?"

"Yes, plenty, but there's not much lamb in it," Kate answered, taking two bowls off the shelf and filling them with stew. "You'll find spoons in the drawer."

"Where's the sink? I need to wash my hands."

"No running water. Just pour some water from the pitcher into the basin."

"Good God, this is primitive. I can't believe that there are still places like this in Dublin. Where are the toilet facilities?"

"At the far end of the lane in front of the shower stalls."

"Ugh, outdoor showers in winter!"

"Well, for sixpence, a warm shower, plus soap and a towel is provided at the Tara Street bath house. Of course, it's a men's facility. There isn't such a place for women."

"Aw, just like the street toilets, which are only for men."

"It's not only in Ireland, Sheila. It's like that all over Europe, well in France and England for sure."

"Do you think that's the way it is in America?"

"I have no idea. That matter never came up in *Little Women* or *Gone with the Wind* or any other books about America that I've read," Kate laughed.

"I passed a water tap on my way here. Why are the toilets on one end and the water tap on the opposite end?"

"I don't know who came up with that poor design. The people here are living like our parents and grandparents did."

"Even our grandparents didn't share toilets with non-family members! This is too primitive for me. Do I need to go to the water tap to discard this water?"

"No, there's a circle of stones in the yard. Just throw the water there. There's earth under the stones for the water to sink down into."

"Francis must be a very neat fellow. This place is spotless," Sheila commented. "When does he arrive home?"

"Francis doesn't live here anymore."

"I'm confused. He didn't mention that to me when I was at the farm. You were dating Browne, and you're now living in Egan's cottage?"

"Yes. I thought I loved Harry and believed he loved me. It was all an illusion. Although he never actually said he loved me, he was talking about plans for our marriage and of buying a house. He had it all planned, and he showed me a house that he knew for a fact, he said, would be up for sale in the next couple of months. The owners were planning to move to Austria. He said it would be our house.

"When I told him I was pregnant, he was unpleasantly surprised. He said I, being a nurse, should have handled that end of things. He asked why I wasn't on the pill. How would I have access to it? It's illegal here.

"'That has never stopped anyone from getting the damn pill,' he said. 'London's a 45 minute flight from here. Every girl I know uses it, that is, everyone but you.'

"When he said 'every girl he knows' uses it, I felt a shiver of shame. I was one of the many, and the stupidest of the lot. As though the situation wasn't bad enough as things stood, I made them worse by crying. He then put his arm around me, and said I should give him a few days and he'd leave 'the necessary' in an envelope with the bartender at The Mouse That Roared."

"What necessary?"

"A boat ticket to England, and the name and address of someone who'll take care of things," he said.

"A boat ticket! Not a plane ticket? How very cheap of him!" Sheila injected.

"Yes, a boat trip and an abortion! What he was saying was now becoming clear to me."

"'Don't blame me,' he had answered. 'If you had used protection you wouldn't be in the spot you are.' Then he left."

"Did you go to The Mouse That Roared?"

"Yes, but I didn't speak to the bartender. I couldn't go that route. Instead I saw a man sitting alone on a bar stool and went over and sat on the empty stool next to him. I began a conversation, which was difficult. He was definitely a man of few words and with none to spare. With prodding from me, we met again the next evening I had off. After I'd been seeing him for almost three weeks, I prolonged the evening and told him I'd just missed the last bus back to my flat. Francis said he had his van outside and would drive me there."

"So you picked the most handsome fellow in the bar?"

"I picked someone who appeared to be the most approachable man there, and one who was alone. Francis was the opposite of Harry, who had pressured me into my first sexual encounter. It was I who enticed Francis. I did a dreadful thing to him by passing off the parentage of the child from Harry to Francis. I couldn't bring myself to destroy a life, and I needed a name for this child and a birth certificate that hadn't 'illegitimate' stamped across it."

"Harry treated you horribly!" Sheila said between spoonfuls of stew.

"That was not a good reason for me to have treated Francis so shamefully. Word got to Francis that it was Harry who had impregnated me. It was, in all probability, Harry who told Francis. Francis walked out, not to return."

"You must hate them both."

"Harry wasn't the person I thought him to be. I was so naïve. I was merely caught up in Harry's words and plans for us, and the illusion of love. Francis is an honest and decent person; I was his illusion. I destroyed his trust in me just as I realized I loved him."

"Maybe he'll come back. It is his house!"

"No, he won't be back. I remember how he looked when he left." A silence fell.

"You've made a great stew, Kate. Francis is missing out on a scrumptious meal," Sheila lightly added, to soften the dense air that clamped down around them. "I'll spend the night, if you'd like me to."

"Thank you, Sheila that would be great."

"They haven't allowed you to continue working at the hospital, have they?"

"No, I had to resign when I got pregnant."

"Yes, the hospital's idiotic rule."

"I could have managed to have worked much longer since I didn't show. It was the morning sickness, I believe, that gave me away. I don't know why it's called morning sickness, as it stuck around until mid afternoon. I couldn't eat until about three o'clock in the afternoon, and then I was ravenously hungry. When the Mother Superior called me into her office, I knew it was a bad omen. She wouldn't even let me finish the week. I knew I was clutching at straws when I asked if I could work in the nursery. After all, babies wouldn't object to my pregnancy, but she told me that wasn't an option. She accused me of being underhanded by not following the hospital rules and informing her of my condition immediately."

CHAPTER 3

Sitting before a breakfast of rashers and eggs, tea and scones, Sheila asked, "What are your plans after the baby is born? Do you intend to continue living here?"

"I don't have much choice. Soon I'll have an infant to take care of. This is a safe place to raise a child, and I've grown attached to this cottage of inconveniences."

"You could sell it and move into a flat with all amenities."

"Sell this cottage! No. Beside this is still Francis' cottage, and it certainly is that in the eyes of the lane people."

"Is it also that you're hoping Francis will come back?"

"There is a bit of that. However, if Francis is to come back, it won't be for me. That's over and done with as far as he's concerned. Then, of course, he could come back to sell the cottage! He's not living here, why should he not sell the cottage?"

"Don't even think that. You're one of the more fortunate ones, Kate. You're pregnant and living in Dublin and accountable to nobody, rather than in some small town where you would be unable to keep your baby."

"Why wouldn't I be able to keep it?"

"Most unwed mothers don't have that option."

"They don't?"

"Kate, you remember Nancy from back home?"

"Nancy, who lived across from Leary's pub? Yes, I do remember her. She had a very strange mother. After Nancy left to stay with her aunt in Cork, I asked her mother for Nancy's address so I could write to her. Her mother said, 'If Nancy wished to keep in touch with me, she knew where I lived,' then rudely added, 'Nancy would be making a whole lot of new friends in Cork.'"

"O Lord, Kate, think about it. We knew Nancy all our lives. She never spoke of an aunt in Cork, nor did she or her family ever visit Cork in all the years we had known her, until the day she suddenly left. Doesn't that seem strange to you?"

"Why would she say she was going to visit her aunt in Cork if she wasn't?"

"I need another cup of tea. Kate, the flame on this stove has gone down." Kate put two shillings in the gas meter and the flame rose. When the water came to a boil, Sheila added water to the tea leaves and let it steep. "More tea for you, Kate?"

After pouring the tea, Sheila addressed the subject.

"Nancy was pregnant."

"She was? Did she have a boy or a girl?"

"Whatever she had doesn't matter. Nancy was sent to one of those homes for unwed mothers to have her baby. The child would have been put up for adoption, and she'd never again see it."

"What if Nancy wanted to keep her baby?"

"Pregnant girls in these homes don't have that choice. The children are taken from them. They have no say in the matter."

"That's horrible," Kate said with a look of sorrow crossing her face.

"Ignorance and intolerance is what is horrible."

"You're only three years older than me. How do you know so much about these things?"

"My father, the politician. No, not directly from him did I get the information. My eavesdropping began by accident after I overheard my father and the others, those who rule their very small corner of the world, speak of pregnant girls being discreetly hustled off to have their babies, who would be given up for adoption. My father thought I was engrossed in a book on Thursday evenings when he and his colleagues met. That, however, was when I would listen in on their conversation." Sheila brought Kate into a world Kate had never known existed.

"After the war," Sheila continued, "there were hundred of thousands of displaced orphans in Europe. It started with the American G.I. Then Americans in general began adopting Italian, French, German, and English children. Americans were seen not only as the liberators of Europe, they soon became the saviors of the abandoned orphans the war produced by adopting them."

"Why did they not adopt American children from orphanages in America? Remember that film, we saw called 'Boys Town' with Spencer Tracy?"

"Yes."

"That was a place for homeless boys. I figure they must have had a similar place for orphan girls," Kate suggested.

"I believed Americans wanted to adopt babies, not older children, and European children appealed to them."

Sheila drank some tea.

"After the war, Germany immediately began to rebuild. Women, young and old, and every child of school age, and whatever men were available, joined in scraping off bricks from bomb-demolished buildings and placing them in a pile for reuse. Then a lorry would come, the people would put them in, and the bricks would be driven to a building site. Soon the German government prohibited the adoption of their children by non-German people. Like Germany, France and other countries having suffered huge population losses as a result of the war, moved to protect their children, setting up regulations which would prevent outside adoption of their young citizens.

"I think it was 1948 when the UK forbade foreign nationals from adopting British children. Americans turned to Ireland, just a short flight away, and it became a happy hunting ground for well-to-do Americans and sometimes for people who wanted to hold their marriage together. These Irish babies were classified as war orphans, yet Ireland had been neutral throughout WWII."

"So why did we let ours be adopted?"

"Poverty," Sheila answered. "Now in the '50s it isn't much better but in the '40s, Ireland was a desolate country. Because of her neutrality, Ireland alone did not share in any of the huge sums of money America poured into the postwar development of Europe. Ireland was predominantly rural. Church and State, hand in hand, ruled the country and enforced its strict moral code. Chastity was demanded of everyone who wasn't married. Of course, women alone paid the price for their indiscretions. High unemployment and low wages kept the marriage rate woefully low. Men simply couldn't afford to take wives and children. With Ireland's poor economy, the government could ill support those children who should not, according to our moral code, have existed. Our government continued to export children for adoption overseas even at a time of mass emigration and a declining population. Once started, it was difficult to stop."

"Why didn't the mothers protest?"

"In our male-oriented society? " Sheila gave a bitter laugh. "There was an appalling stigma attached to illegitimacy, thereby forcing the women to join the Church and government in concealment, deception and denial. Even the girls' families were scandalized by a pregnancy before marriage."

"I, too, concealed and deceived. My family still doesn't know I'm pregnant."

"You were fortunate, Kate, in that you were not in a small town when it happened. Dublin was always more open, more cosmopolitan. Where we lived, girls never got pregnant. They went to visit a relative, when in actuality, they entered homes for unwed mothers. These homes have a frightening reputation, and young girls are punished for their 'sins' by cleaning and scrubbing in these homes or working the land.

"The authorities frequently disposed of children without consulting or informing the mother beforehand. Other times, they were told people would be arriving to look over the babies, and that they should wash them and dress them in the new clothes they were given on such occasions."

"Why didn't these women run away from those horrible places?" asked Kate.

"They weren't permitted beyond the gates. Some did try to escape but were always brought back by the police. And if they had succeeded, where would they have found sanctuary?"

"What happened to the women after their babies were taken from them? Where did they go?"

"Some married and had other children without ever telling their husbands about the baby that had been taken from them because their shame was so great. That hidden secret took a heavy toll. Others went overseas to work and built lives in exile. Some, however, never left the place of their imprisonment, never recovered psychologically from their experience and were never able to restart their lives."

Kate now understood her mother's actions, yet she realized it was people who thought like her mother that helped this sorry plight exist for so many unfortunate women. Sheila had not only pushed Kate out of her own cocoon but made her realize how very fortunate she was. If she ever saw Francis again, she would thank him from the bottom of her heart.

She was sorry to see Sheila leave. Their goodbyes were especially sad since Sheila was leaving the country.

Kate phoned Kieran to inquire about getting a loan on her inheritance, which she would use to pay the taxes on the cottage.

"Well, how is my little sister?"

"I'm fine thanks. How are you? Breda and the children?"

Kieran went into great details about his two young children. When Kate could get a word in edgeways, before running out of coins, she mentioned that she wanted an advance on her inheritance. Since her brother handled all the family's legal affairs with the man who had been their father's lawyer, perhaps he could speak to the lawyer concerning her request.

"Are we being cut off?"

"No. I've put in some more coins."

"Well, since you don't have a telephone, I'll get your address from Mom, and get back to you on this matter."

"No, she doesn't have my address."

"She must. You sent her something. Yes, I remember, a card for her birthday. It's good to know you're all right. Glad you called. You really should get a phone installed, Kate. These pay phones are a terrible inconvenient method of communication. I'll be in touch. Bye."

She had purposely refrained from putting her address on the card she had sent her mother. She would call Kieran back in a week. By that time he would know their mother didn't have the address, and he might also have Dad's lawyer's response to her request. She would bring a fist full of coins with her. Of course, the details on all his daughters' activities took time to relate, and the interruptions of inserting coins had kept him from asking her why she needed the money. On the next phone call, she knew, she would have to answer that question.

A week later, Kate telephoned Kieran. After saying he hoped she was well, Kieran became very businesslike. He had spoken to the lawyer who was adamant in his response that the money could not be touched before its due date. Kieran wanted to know if she was living beyond her means! If so, he could go over her expenses and set a budget for her. If her finances were out of control, he urged her to come home until they were settled.

She was well, she assured him. Although disappointed that she could not draw on her inheritance, she told him she could manage. Would he have suggested she return home if he knew she was pregnant? Did he think she was so frivolous as to make a request for this money if it were not an emergency? His attitude angered her so much she shortened the conversation for fear of revealing too much and saying something she might later regret.

Kate sold her watch and used that money and the remainder of her bank account to pay the tax bill on the cottage.

A fortnight later, Kate received a very brief letter from Francis indicating he was leaving the country the following morning. He wished her well in all her endeavors and signed it simply, Francis.

With the Metropole Cinema want advertisement in her hand, Kate applied for a job as a cleaning woman. It was a rainy day, and, wearing Francis's shirt under her beltless raincoat to hide her expanding stomach, she was hired.

All the cleaning women were considerably older than Kate, and they were aware of her advanced pregnancy. She joined the wave of women going from row to row of seats, constantly stooping to pick up candy wrappers, used food containers and other rubbish from between and under the seats as they hurried ahead of the male workers who came after them, vacuuming the carpeting. Other women cleaned the restrooms. Every other week, the women switched tasks.

These women were mostly from a permanently poor class of people; some were single and others were married women with children, some of whom were near Kate's age. They were a most cheerful group of women with keen wit and a lively sense of humor. They brought plenty of food for their mid-morning break, which they insisted on sharing with Kate. When she politely refused their generosity, they would insist, saying it was for the baby.

After working a month, Mr. Caulfield, the cinema manager who had hired Kate called her into his office. To her relief, she was not being dismissed. One of the ticket sellers had to leave her job temporarily to take care of her sick father. Kate was being asked to sell tickets at the booth in front of the cinema. She gratefully accepted the job.

Kate wondered how the cleaning women knew she was being offered the ticket-selling position before she got the job. She discovered that when they had found it was available, each of them in turn had passed it up with the suggestion that Kate be chosen. When she returned from Mr. Caulfield's office to tell them the news, they had a surprise party awaiting her. Along with their mid-morning tea was a store-bought cake and individual tubs of ice cream from the cinema's concession stand. They had obtained permission to purchase the ice cream while the stand was closed, when a film was not being shown.

The cleaning women, whom Kate had grown very fond of, came to her booth to hand in their weekly movie passes in exchange for tickets. In the process, Kate met their husbands, children and sometimes their grandchildren. They kept her informed of all the happenings in their lives: a son imprisoned for stealing a car without knowing how to drive. He was fine; the car was not! Seven- and nine-year-old grandchildren who couldn't be found long after their bedtime. The police being notified, and then the children wandered home after the greyhound races were over. Mishaps were told with great humor, as was gossip. Her new friends were concerned for Kate and looked forward to the arrival of her baby. They did not tell her, but knowing their betting habits, she knew that each of them, and most likely the men cleaners as well, would have placed bets on the day the baby would be born. This made Kate smile, and she wondered who would win the bet.

Kate worked in the cinema until two days before her delivery.

CHAPTER 4

When the women of the lane became aware of her pregnancy, they stopped her to ask how she was feeling, spoke of the unborn baby, and offered advice, always addressing her as Mrs. Egan. They were curious as to where Francis had gone, and why he had left. But, of course, nobody would ask. They rightly assumed she was working and wrongly assumed she had an office job. They never asked about her family, and Kate did not offer any information. They slowly became her friends, and their friendship lightened her load.

Passing by the Egan cottage early on a Saturday morning, Kathleen Purdy heard a low moan. She stopped, put her water pail down and listened. Mentally calculating the months, she thought, 'No it can't be her time. It's too early.' Then on hearing a muffled cry, Kathleen opened the cottage door and walked in calling out, "Mrs. Egan."

On hearing movement in the bedroom, Kathleen walked towards it and saw Kate in the process of delivering a child. "Good God," Kathleen exclaimed, "I didn't think you were ready. I'll run up the lane and get Tara." Before Kate could stop her, Kathleen was out the door and soon knocking on Tara Mulcahy's door. Moments later the two women entered Kate's cottage to find the child in bed with its mother.

Tara had brought a kettle of boiling water that was meant for her husband's breakfast. On seeing Kate and the newborn child nestled against her, Tara put down the kettle and hurried to the bedside.

"The baby! It arrived without a pip out of you!" Tara exclaimed. Then picking up the infant she held it upside down, and it gave out a lusty cry. This sound brought smiles to the women's faces. They examined him and declared him a beautiful, healthy boy.

"Peg is the midwife, Mrs. Egan. However, Peg and her husband have gone to stay with their daughter and her family for the weekend to celebrate her grandson's confirmation," Kathleen explained.

"We'll manage," Kate assured her.

"This water is too hot to wash him?" Tara noted.

"Take some of the cold water from the covered pot on the stove. It has been boiled." Kate said. Then turning to Kathleen added, "If you'll put some of the boiling water into the large dish on the table, I'll drop in the scissors to sterilize them and cut the umbilical cord."

"Cut the cord!" Kathleen faintly repeated as she placed the scissors in a shallow dish and covered them with boiling water.

"My name is Kate."

"I'm Tara, and this is Kathleen."

"Hand me the dish, Kathleen, and I'll cut the cord."

When Kathleen had done as Kate asked, Kate with steady hands cut the cord and knotted it firmly close to the baby's belly. Tara combined some hot and cold water, and taking the child, washed him and wrapped him in a large towel while Kathleen attended to Kate, removing all the blood-soaked newspapers Kate had earlier sterilized. She put them in a bag to be discarded and then helped wash the new mother.

"When did your labor start?" Tara asked as she placed the infant in Kate's arms.

"About eleven o'clock last night."

"Why didn't you call one of us last night? You shouldn't have been alone at a time like this."

"We go through birth and death alone, even if surrounded by people."

"Well, you have a point there, Kate," Tara agreed." We're alone in the sense that nobody can do it for us. I've never knotted an umbilical cord. Peg always took care of that. I was just her assistant. The last baby born in these cottages was the Walsh baby, and she is now nine years old. I'm certainly glad you were able to cut the cord."

"How do you know how to do all this?"

"I'm a nurse."

"Aw," both women smiled as they said,"A nurse!"

"We certainly could use a nurse here in the lane," Kathleen assured Kate.

Hearing voices from the Egan cottage, other neighboring women came into the house. Tara addressed them."Kate just gave birth to a beautiful baby boy. Kate, this is Sioban, Lil, Monica and Ruth. Ladies, meet Kate."

"Kate," Siobhan smiled. "I wondered what you were called. We all did. We saw you coming and going but hadn't the nerve to ask."

"Why not?"

"Well, you're kind of different."

"You're a cut above us, is what Siobhan means."

"Lil, you're making a hash of things. Many of us, Kate, haven't gone beyond the eighth class and some of us only made it to the sixth class before leaving school. I began work in the jam factory when I was fourteen and worked there until I married," Monica explained.

"This is my home."

"That it is, Kate. You're one of us, even more so now since your son has been born in the lane," Ruth assured Kate. All expressed agreement.

"Do you have a name for this fine young fellow?"

"Yes, I'll call him Eoin after my father. Eoin Francis," Kate replied, rapidly choosing a name. Francis' absence was the huge elephant in the room that all tried to ignore. What could she say? She did not care to enlighten these good people to her sorry state of affairs.

Someone, that day several months ago, saw her run after Francis to plead with him not to leave. One person would have made it known to all. She hoped they wouldn't think badly of Francis for leaving her. Would they treat her son differently if they knew the circumstances of his conception? They would be aghast, she believed, by her deception. Could she have revealed these hidden lies and continued to live in the lane? Sheila, the one person she could confide in was now living overseas.

"Eoin Francis. That's a fine name."

"Will you have him baptized in St. Patrick's?"

"No, I'll have him baptized in the church in Swords where Francis and I were married," Kate answered with a slight hesitation. The elephant was growing bigger and was consuming all the air in the room. For a few tense moments, silence prevailed.

"Will Francis come home for the Baptism?" Tara ventured to ask.

"No."

"Is it to England he has gone?"

"Yes," Kate answered, not knowing where he had gone. Another lie added to the heap.

"Well, working his uncle's farm was fine when there was just himself. Working that small farm wouldn't support a wife and child. It's just enough to give his aunt and uncle a modest living," Sioban surmised.

"Maybe he'll return for the child's first birthday," Lil smiled.

So that was the conclusion they had come to. I wonder where in the world he is. I'm one of them now, a lane person, accepted, as is my son. Eoin will grow up in the same house as Francis had. Intentional or not, it was cruel of him to omit from his letter where he was going. Not intentional, she decided, partially because he was not a person given to cruelty, and partially because carelessness on his part was easier to deal with than intent. She had no way to contact him. *Perhaps he will contact me when he is settled in a new job and has place to live. Would Francis return? What are his intentions? Not knowing made everything tentative.*

"I was wondering, do you need to borrow a pram, or might there be one in your family you wish to use?" Tara asked.

This was the first time anyone in the lane mentioned the possibility that she might have a family. She'd like to say, 'Oh yes, ladies, my brother has two young daughters who had a fine baby carriage, bought by my mother, but my son being born out of wedlock is hidden from them.'

"No. I am without a pram."

"Well, my daughter has one you can borrow. I asked her ahead of time in the event that you might not have one."

"Thank you, and please thank your daughter for me."

"My son Terry and his wife had three boys, so if you wouldn't mind having a crib that has had a bit of rough treatment, you're very welcome to it. It is quite sturdy, which it would have to be to withstand those holy terrors."

"Thanks, Lil. Thank you all for all your kindness." Kate looked around the room at each and every one of these good people. In silence they acknowledged her gratitude. A little awkward, they stood, unfamiliar with praise, yet proud to have been a part of this event. Then they smiled and hugged Kate and each other.

"Welcome, baby Eoin. You have brought much joy into our lives," Kathleen, speaking for all, stated.

"Yes. Kate and this precious child are part of all our lives here in the lane," Monica added.

The room that had grown solemn became full of smiles, and those gathered were moved to tears, until Kathleen spoke.

"How come you so conveniently had water boiling when I knocked at your door, Tara?"

"That was for Frank's tea." Then remembering she added, "Good Lord, he hasn't had a cup of tea yet!"

"Well, surely he can make himself a cup of tea," Ruth laughed.

"Not without a tea kettle," Kathleen joined in the laughter.

"You go along and make him breakfast," Kate urged.

"Go ahead, Tara. I'll make Kate some tea."

"Kate will need more than tea in order to feed that young fellow. I'll be making stew today, and I'll bring some over," Tara said as she headed out the door with her tea kettle.

"I'll be cooking a ham for Sunday's dinner, so I'll bring some over tomorrow, with potatoes, parsnips and turnips," Monica said.

Ruth who had slipped out unnoticed by all, returned with a pail of water. She overheard Monica and asked if Kate liked shepherd's pie. Then asked what days were covered.

"You'll be Monday," Lil answered and set herself for Tuesday's dinner. Kathleen took Wednesday and Friday and would cook fish on both days. Siobhan agreed to Thursday saying she wasn't as good a cook as the other ladies but could manage to fry some lamb chops with chips.

"I'm going to make a couple of poached eggs for Kate to have with her tea, and all you ladies must leave for now and let her get some sleep. She has had a long night," Kathleen stated.

"I'll pop in tomorrow morning before going to the market to see what you need, Kate," and having said that, Monica bid Kate good-bye.

Each of the women took another look at the baby, agreed with each other that he was a most beautiful child, praised Kate for her good work, and left.

Alone in the cottage, Kate looked at the child lying beside her and softly told him, "You're your grandmother's first grandson. You have two cousins, Deirdre who is two years old, and Nora four. One day I'm going to have to explain a lot of things to you but not until you are much older. Ned and Mary will be the first relatives you'll be introduced to. Depending on the outcome, you will or will not have family close by. Well, Eoin, since you've closed your eyes and gone to sleep, I'll assume you don't wish to hear anymore about family ties at the moment."

She had told the women she would have her son baptized in the chapel wherein she and Francis had made their vows, 'Love, honor and obey—in sickness, and in health as long as you both shall live.' Nothing in that ceremony covered events that occurred before marriage.

Lies. I am heartfelt sorry. What had Francis told Ned and Mary? Had he revealed all to them? Would she and the child be welcomed, or told never again to darken their doorstep? In a few weeks she would walk the five miles, with Eoin, from the bus stop to the farm. Then she would bring Eoin to the cinema and introduce him to the cleaning women, supplying the time and date of birth so that their bets could be honored.

Closing her eyes, Kate, exhausted, fell asleep and dreamt. On a bright sunny day, Kate and Francis walked hand in hand along the Dodder River. They stopped and looked at the swans below gracefully gliding along.

"Swans always seemed magical to me. Maybe it's because I

loved hearing my father read *The Children of Lir* and how his four children were turned into swans by their stepmother."

"Swans mate for life," Francis told her.

"Yes, so I've been told."

As she looked over the wall, Kate bent over to pick the wildflowers growing on the riverside. She had picked just a few when she noticed a dark cloud suddenly sweep over the water. She shivered. Turning from the river, she sought Francis but instead another person stood where Francis had stood—a dark brooding figure whose face was partly turned from her and hidden by his wide upturned collar. Francis was nowhere in sight. Dismayed, she dropped the flowers. The man stooped to pick them up. Terror seized her. She tried to run but could not. Kate woke in panic. She was disoriented. A sudden, loud, frightened cry from Eoin brought her back in time and place.

She wrapped the eiderdown from the bed around her as she walked over to Eoin, picked him up, held him to her breast and folded him into the eiderdown. Soon he stopped crying and went back to sleep. Sleep eluded Kate.

Kate was anxious to know if she and Eoin would be welcomed at Ned and Mary's home. In mid-November, when Eoin was three weeks old, they set out on their journey to Swords. After a fifteen-minute wait, they boarded a bus for the fifteen-minute ride into the city. They then waited forty minutes for the bus from the city to the farm. It was a cold windy day in spite of the bright sun. Eoin grew restless as they waited. Kate wheeled the pram one bus length, back and forth, until he fell asleep. As she walked, she wondered whether Ned and Mary would add to her skimpy knowledge of Francis' whereabouts. She had not seen either of them since her wedding day. She would have liked to phone them before making this trip, but they had no telephone. Now that Eoin was asleep, she sat on the bench at the bus stop and opened her book: Joyce's short story, *The Dead*, where Gretta, on hearing a song at a New Year's Eve party she was attending with her husband, Gabriel, is brought back in time to the death of her first love. Her husband, seeing the love and longing in her eyes, misunderstands. Kate abruptly let go of Gabriel's rejection and pain as the bus pulled up in front of them.

After alighting from the bus in Swords, Kate looked around the town that she and Francis had passed through in happier times. *Perhaps I have made a mistake in coming. If my own family would not accept this child, whatever made me believe Francis' family would? Am I expecting too much from these two kind people?* She wanted to get back on the return bus to the city, but scolded herself, '*you have come all this way; finish the journey.*' And so, she took the road that led to the farm. What seemed like a short ride in the van proved to be a fifty-minute walk! They had left the lane shortly before nine that morning, and it would be close to one o'clock when they arrived at the farm. Eoin grew hungry and protested with a strong cry. Kate sat by the side of this lonely road, leaned back into the blackberry bushes, and with the carriage blanket around both her and the child, she nursed him. When Eoin was satisfied, they resumed their journey.

Coming out of the barn, Ned was the first to see them walk through the gate. He smiled at them in greeting, and coming forward, said, "It's good to see you again, Kate. So this is the child?"

"Yes, this is Eoin Francis."

"He's a fine big fellow. It'll be a few years yet before he'll be riding a horse. Do you ride, Kate?"

"Not for several years, but when growing up, I was never happier than on horseback."

"Then you must ride our horses, and Eoin, too, when he is ready," Ned concluded. Remembering how anxious Mary was to see the child and its mother, he concluded, "I'll be in a heap of trouble if Mary sees me out here delaying you from entering the house." He called Mary's name. She came out of the house drying her hands on her apron.

"As I live and breathe, it's you, Kate, and the baby!" Mary uttered in joy as she flung her hands upwards. On reaching Kate, she hugged her. "Come into the house before the wind blows us all away," and she hastened them indoors. "Did you walk from the town?"

"Yes."

"Oh child, why didn't you let us know? Ned could have picked you up at the bus stop."

"You don't have a phone."

"The pub in town does! Kate, you can always leave a message there for us. Ned goes into town every morning with the milk churns. If you need to get in touch at any other time, don't hesitate to call. Mr. Moore will send one of the lads out to the farm to deliver it. I'll write down the number for you."

"We were fortunate. A few dark clouds gathered overhead, but it didn't rain, and the sun soon came through."

Mary, looking down at the sleeping child, asked, "Is it a boy or girl?"

"A boy, Eoin Francis. Not yet official. He hasn't been baptized. I'd like to have him baptized in the small stone church where Francis and I were married," Kate watched Mary's face as she mentioned Francis' name.

"What happened, Kate? Why did Francis leave, especially when you were pregnant?"

"He didn't tell you?"

"He told us he was leaving and would look for a job in England."

Jumping on this bit of information, her mind ran on. *He is in England! Should I ask for his address? Why? He must not want me to write him.*

"He refused to discuss it further. It is most unlike Francis to behave in this manner, especially now that he has a wife and child. I cannot understand his actions. I know the farm doesn't pay much. On hearing Francis was leaving, Ned offered to sign the farm over to Francis, and Ned would work for him. Francis thanked him, but refused to enter into that arrangement. It will be Francis' farm after we are gone, Ned argued, so why not take it now and run it in whatever manner he wished? But Francis wouldn't hear of it. I'd never seen him as happy as when he told us he had met you and wanted to marry you. How then could he have done this?" Mary shook her head in disbelief and waved her hands in a gesture of despair.

"It wasn't Francis' fault. It was mine."

"What could you have done, child, to create this situation?" Mary added, dismissing the idea.

"Something I'm ashamed of. I've been holding onto this secret for so long without telling a soul, other than my cousin Sheila who is now in England."

"Let me make us a cup of tea. Dinner won't be ready for another hour."

"I may not be invited to dinner, or permitted to visit the farm after what I'm about to tell you."

Over several cups of tea, Kate told Mary the whole story. When she had finished, she awaited Mary's verdict.

"He loved you, Kate. Knowing that, did you not believe he would have accepted the child as his own?"

"Now, yes. Back then, no! I had thought another man loved me, but when he found me pregnant with his child, he became a whole different person. I wasn't ready to trust again."

Ned entered the house. "So good to see you again, Kate, and I hope we'll see a lot more of you and the lad."

"I'll have dinner on the table in no time at all." Rising, Mary readied the meal for serving as Kate put the plates and cutlery on the table. "After dinner, Kate and I will make a visit to see Father Brendan to arrange Eoin's baptism."

On the way to the church, Mary wished to know who the godparents would be. Kate had her cousin in mind as godmother in absentia. No godfather had been picked, as yet. On hearing this, Mary suggested Ned be considered.

"I know he's old for such a position, but he would be honored to be asked, and we both will love and care for the child as though he were our own flesh and blood."

"Then it's settled. I will ask Ned to be godfather, and you, Mary, and my cousin as godmothers."

A few hours later, as they prepared to leave, Mary and Ned expressed the hope that Kate and Eoin would spend Christmas with them. Mary wrapped ham, fresh vegetables, homemade bread, eggs, and apple pie into a box for Kate to take home with her. Ned drove them to the bus stop and put the carriage and box onto the bus. When Kate arrived in the city and alighted from the bus, she put the box in the carriage and carried Eoin to the next bus stop and then to the lane. She would return in a fortnight to have Eoin baptized.

"Well, Eoin, love, we now know, you are fortunate to have two wonderful people as family."

CHAPTER 5

Walking into church with Ned and Mary to have her son baptized, Kate suddenly became overwhelmed with a sense of guilt and failure. Last spring, she and Francis, deliriously happy, had entered this church to make their wedding promises to each other before God and the community. She had ruined everything! Francis, apparently, felt he had to leave the country of his birth to distance himself from her. She did not believe he could ever again love her, but she needed to know if he could forgive her. Mary said Francis would have accepted Eoin as his son. She unwittingly drove Francis away and deprived Eoin of a father. She wondered if Francis and Eoin would get to know each other or even meet one another. Had she made a mistake in having him baptized in this church of their beautiful memories?

With tears in her eyes, Kate handed the child to Mary and headed downstairs to the ladies room. After composing herself, she returned. Although she had not received permission from Francis to do so, the child was baptized Eoin Francis Egan, and the record would show Francis Egan as the child's father.

Arriving home shortly after seven o'clock in the evening on the day Eoin was baptized, Kate, emotionally drained from the day's ordeal, put her son in the crib and took off her coat. A noise outside her door was followed by a soft knock. Kate opened it slowly and saw the cheerful faces of her neighbors.

"Well, has he been duly baptized?" Monica smiled.

"We've come with something a bit stronger than water!" Tara said, not waiting for Kate to answer Monica's question as they walked in, followed by other neighboring women and their husbands carrying platters of sandwiches, cake, and an assortment of bottles. Soon Jameson's, soda water, wine, Guinness, and lemonade were opened and poured by the men and passed around. Each woman put several shillings into the folds of the baby's blanket, as was the custom.

"We've been waiting and watching for your return," Lil answered the surprised look on Kate's face.

"To Eoin: may you have good health and a long life." Tara's husband John toasted. All drank.

"Sláinte" was spoken in unison.

When the party was in full swing, a bearded old man walked in the partly opened door carrying a bottle of brandy. A silence fell on the room like a hammer. Kathleen's husband spoke into the silence, "Can I pour you some Jameson's?"

"Aye, indeed," the old man answered with a nod. He drank the Jameson's and held out his glass again. When his glass was refilled, the old man walked towards the crib. "To the child," he stated as he raised his glass. All glasses were again raised in a toast, after which the old man held the glass over the child for several moments as his lips moved but no sound was heard. Then he drank, emptying the glass and turned to leave. Kate followed him to the door and thanked him for coming and offering a blessing upon the child, although she had no idea who he was or what he had said. Turning to her, as he placed his hand on the doorknob, he asked, "Are you Francis' wife?"

"Yes. I have seen you on two or three occasions in the lane, so I gather you know Francis."

"Aye, indeed, very well. Is it to England he's gone?"

"Yes."

He seemed to reflect on some matter for a moment or two, then spoke.

"That's a fine young lad you've got. He's the image of yourself."

"So I've been told."

As he walked out the door, he turned and added with a vague smile and a twinkle in his eye, "No red hair."

"No, no red hair," she smiled back at him.

"Thank you," he added from the lane, and then he was gone.

No red hair! For a second or two Kate wondered if the old man possessed information none of the other guests had. Kate then scolded herself for such thinking. *Don't get paranoid about events that have happened.* Kate wondered why she was being thanked. It could not have been for an invitation to come tonight for none were extended. The door was open to all who wished to enter. For some unknown reason she felt happy that this man with the unruly beard and deep all-knowing eyes had made an appearance. She would not discuss their brief exchange of words with the women. Although she did not understand why he had come or why he had said what he did, she knew it was meant for her alone.

"That's Old Man O'Toole," Lil whispered to Kate although he was well on his way to his own cottage by that time.

"What possessed that old codger to come?" one of the men asked in surprise.

"He never shows up at any event," his wife added.

Soon the men, having toasted the child, left the women to linger while they headed for the local pub.

"Old O left his unopened bottle of brandy here," Siobhan said in merriment.

"Well he might. I hear that old recluse is loaded with money."

"I didn't see him part with any of it to the child," Tara laughed.

"That's all a rumor. Why would he be living in the lane if he had money?" Monica wanted to know.

"He's living here, no doubt, because he doesn't want to spend any of it." Kathleen laughed.

"He must be sixty if he's a day. He never married. He had one brother who, for all any of us know, may be dead and gone. None have ever visited him, so why would he be holding onto it if he had money?" Monica questioned the group.

"That's what misers do. They hold onto every penny they've got," Siobhan explained.

"That doesn't make sense, and he with no family to leave it to," Monica said shaking her head, "and he on his last lap around."

"Well, if he has any money, he certainly spends as little as possible," Lil commented.

"He brought brandy here tonight," Kate smiled.

"That he did. Now, that was a big surprise," Tara said.

"The biggest surprise is that he showed up at all," Peg added to the amusement of all.

"Why did he, and he a recluse, wander in here tonight?" Monica wondered.

"There's no knowing what people will do," Peg added, and the discussion on Mr. O'Toole came to an end as the conversation took a new direction.

Kate and Eoin were ready early on the morning of Christmas Eve to make the trip to the farm. It was the first time Kate had felt sorrow instead of joy at Christmastime. She thought of her mother, Kieran and family, Rory and his wife, Gwen, her extended family of uncles, aunts, and cousins sitting down for dinner on Christmas Day, laughing, eating, and talking among much merriment. They would probably mention her briefly and then dismiss her absence from them. She had sent her mother a Christmas card. A handwritten message inviting her home for Christmas had arrived from her mother who was blissfully unaware that she had a grandson.

Kate never did have a rapport with her mother. At times she felt her mother did not really like her. Was that her imagination? Had her mother been severe with her for her own sake? After her father died, she felt like a stranger in her mother's house, so much so that she was happy when the time came to return to boarding school.

As Kate straightened the wedding quilt on the bed, made with loving hands by Mary and her neighbors, her mind wandered to a happier time when she and Francis snuggled together under its warmth. What had Francis planned for this his first Christmas away from home! She knew he would miss his cottage, his uncle and aunt and the farm. How could he not? She felt guilt in knowing that she was the reason he felt he had to leave Dublin. Had his harsh feeling towards her, rightly deserved, subsided?

Eoin, all bundled up for outdoors, became restless.

"It's all right, love, we're leaving."

As she picked up the child and placed him in the pram, she spoke to him, "Francis would love you if only he could see you. You too, Eoin, must endure the results of my 'unsavory past'. I pray that, in the years to come, when you learn all the details, you won't turn against me."

As Kate wheeled the pram towards the door, she saw a piece of mail come into the mail slot. As she picked it up she told the child, "This will only take a moment, Eoin." It looked like a Christmas card, and it had an English postmark. As she opened the envelope she found it did indeed contain a Christmas card, a money order, and a brief message, "Thought you could use some money over the Christmas holidays. Francis." Although she certainly had need of the money, she had an even greater need to know if he was happy at this joyful time of year. What position had he been able to secure? What kind of living accommodations did he have? Was he content living in London? She knew he must miss Ned and Mary. Did he miss her? He had to have thought of her in order to send the card and money order. With a lighter step and a feeling close to joy, Kate left the cottage that morning to spend Christmas at the farm. She could hardly wait to tell Mary and Ned of her surprise Christmas greetings from Francis. The card alone was the best Christmas gift she could have received and the money was an added bonus.

At the farm, Kate found the kind and gentle Ned looking worn by the end of the day. Since Mary delighted in playing with Eoin, Kate asked Ned, as he walked to the cow shed that evening, to instruct her in milking the cows. Under his patient guidance, Kate mastered the milking with only one mishap. While concentrating on the task at hand, she received an unexpected whack on the back of her neck with the cow's tail which caused her to fall forward, toppling the pail and spilling the milk. Fortunately, since there was as yet little in the pail, only a very small amount of milk was spilt.

Christmas at the farm was very pleasant; Kate soon felt quite at home, and found that she hardly thought of her family. To have Francis beside her at the Christmas meal, their first Christmas together, would have been sheer delight. She had held out hope, a false hope, she now realized, that he would return to the farm for Christmas.

Mary, happy to hear Kate had received a Christmas card and money from Francis, exclaimed, "I knew that dear boy would come to his senses." Ned put his hand on Mary's in agreement as they sat at the kitchen table.

"He just needed a bit of time," Ned added.

Kate loved how this couple, who, although greatly saddened by the separation, a separation that caused Francis to leave the country, could love both Francis and her, passing judgment on neither.

Eoin and Kate returned home the day after St. Stephen Day's, Boxing Day in England.

I'm so lonesome for the land, the farm, Mary and Ned, and especially Kate, Francis thought as he walked to his job in a bookstore in London.

The work was interesting and he was among cordial people, both co-workers and customers, but his salary was pitifully small. He had hoped to have money enough saved to send some at Christmastime to Mary and Ned, and to Kate. His salary, however, covered little more than his rent, meals eaten out, since the flat did not have cooking facilities, and other minor expenses. He had bought a suit and new shoes as his position required, and it almost depleted the money he had on arriving in London.

As he ate greasy fish and chips, the most affordable meal available, he longed to be back on the farm where the food was fresh and expertly cooked.

In his dreams, he lay in bed with Kate in the cottage on their wedding night, a night different from previous nights when he was apprehensive. How did it all happen? Would it last? Would she stay? Why would Kate want to share a lifestyle so different from what she was accustomed to? Their wedding night banished all doubts that he had. That night they gave themselves to each other in joyful abandonment, laughter, and happiness greater than either of them had ever known.

Sadly, he lamented, he did not know the time of his visitation. In discovering Kate carried another man's child, a child she presented as his, the news had crushed him so badly he lost faith in her, believing the only reason she consented to marry him was because of her unborn child. It was a disappointment too great for him to bear; their marriage, their love, had no truth to it.

He would have accepted her child. All parts of her were precious to him. She had not loved him enough to confide in him. She chose deception as the cornerstone on which to build their married life, and so it collapsed.

Francis, admittedly, was ashamed of his part in its destruction. In his pain, he acted immaturely. He had not considered it from Kate's perspective. The baby's father obviously rejected her when she told him she was pregnant, Francis now realized. How dreadful she must have felt! Strangely enough, that aspect of this whole affair hadn't dawned on him until this moment, as he walked from the underground to work.

Yet, she chose him that evening, as he ate a sandwich, in the pub. She sat on the bar stool next to him. He smiled at her, and nodded in greeting.

"Does your wife not feed you?" she asked in jest.

"No wife."

"Well, you're fortunate in that this pub serves good grub." He smiled at her statement but did not trust himself to reply. He had not had much experience with women. In fact, he had to sadly admit he knew more about horses and farm animals than he did about women. He wondered, with so many more prosperous looking men in the pub, why did she choose him to converse with? Perhaps she awaited a boyfriend who had been delayed. If this was the situation, he had hoped the delay would be prolonged. He enjoyed her presence, even though he found himself a bit tongue-tied and was glad when silence did not force her to leave. Although he was not drinking anything stronger than tea when she arrived on the scene, he had asked her if she would like a drink. Tea would be nice, she had said. Time passed, and nobody showed up to claim this most attractive creature, and so he suggested they have some wine and sit in one of the nearby booths. She agreed. Time hastened by. It was past the hour he usually retired for the night but this vision sitting across from him seemed immune to the lateness of the hour. She had said she was a nurse. Nurses worked irregular hours attending to patients.

She had missed the bus back to her flat. Only later he would realize this was part of her plan. They both had too much to drink.

Aunt Mary promised him that if Kate got in touch with her and Ned, they would help Kate in every way possible. Mary and Ned saw Kate as the daughter they never had. Poor Mary was tired of waiting for him to find a bride. Kate, too, was very fond of them, and it was Francis' hope that she would contact his aunt and uncle.

People living in the lane would show much kindness to Kate, Francis believed. Kate need not tell them all the details of their brief life together. She was lawfully married. That would make life easier for her and the child, and she had the cottage. When she told the lane people that he had left the country, they would sympathize with her for all of them had a family member or someone close to them who was forced to leave Ireland for employment. This consoled Francis.

"Good morning, Francis," the young woman catching up with him cheerfully addressed him. "I was thinking since you're a bachelor and away from home, and all that, why not join us for Christmas dinner? There's just my mom, dad, my sister and myself. Mom's a real good cook, and she said she'd love to have you join us."

"Thank you, Hazel, for your kind invitation, but I'm not a bachelor. I have a wife and son living in Dublin, and I doubt very much if I'd be good company at this time of year."

Hazel wasn't sure if he actually had a wife, or if he used that as an excuse to turn down her invitation. If he had a wife, why wasn't he returning to Ireland for Christmas? All the Irish go home for Christmas. She was disappointed by his refusal. She had been attracted to him since he arrived at the bookstore. That he ignored her, she attributed to his shyness. She felt a strong attachment to him and the possibility of him having a wife made her quite cross.

"How come all you people leave Ireland and then go around moaning about it? Why leave if you can't be happy anywhere else?"

"A character flaw we all share," he answered lightly and with a smile as he opened the door to the bookstore so she could walk in ahead of him.

"Mr. Egan, may I have a word?" the store manager, Mr. Briggs, beckoned to him as Francis took off his coat. Coming close to Francis, in a chummy fashion, he revealed his need. "Alas, nobody wants to work overtime during Christmas week. The young women dash out of here in the evenings to go Christmas shopping or to Christmas parties. Willis, of course, has to rush home to care for his ailing mother, so I do hope you'll be available for overtime all next week, including all day Saturday which is when we do our biggest sales. You will, of course, get time and a half for Saturday."

When Francis did not reply immediately, Mr. Briggs, added, "I could manage to get you double time for the full day the Saturday before Christmas. Now, Mr. Egan what do you say?"

"I accept, but I'll also need double time for the extra hours on Friday evening."

"Good, I knew I could count on you although you do drive a hard bargain.

You, no doubt, need the extra money to send back to the family in Ireland. Large family is it?"

"My aunt and uncle, my wife and son complete my family."

"Oh! No parents?"

"No, both dead."

Walking away from Mr. Briggs, Francis closed the conversation. Hanging up his mackintosh, he began working.

Walking home that evening, Francis' thoughts weighed heavily on him. He was ashamed of having left Kate. He remembered her bouts of morning sickness. How pale and fragile she appeared, and how she smiled at him when he brought her a cup of tea and dry cream crackers to alleviate its effects. How could he have behaved in such a manner towards Kate? Would she forgive him for abandoning her while she was pregnant and in need of him? Would she happily receive him if he returned, or would she want nothing to do with him? The latter possibility made it difficult for him to return to the lane. Now he had a dream, a hope, whereas if he was to return and Kate rejected him, he would lose even that hope. For now, he would hold onto the dream.

How was she coping financially? He liked his job, but it did not compensate him sufficiently. In the New Year he would begin looking for a better paying position, preferably one that would offer overtime. He must earn more and save enough money to provide properly for Kate and the child before even thinking about returning to the lane, like Mr. O'Toole, of whom it was said, had made his fortunate before returning home. Francis' hope was not that high. Just a decent amount of money to buy a nice home and to have a little money in the bank was what he aspired to. This became his focus, and it made his lonesomeness for the lane, the cottage, for Kate more bearable.

On New Year's Eve, the women of the lane urged Kate, "Don't go to bed until we wish you a Happy New Year on the stroke of midnight. Kate duly remained awake reading until moments before twelve as she waited for the clock to strike the midnight hour.

Into the darkened and still night, a peal of church bells rang out followed by the dull hollow sound of foghorns from the harbor. People from the lane came out of their homes. When Kate opened her door she was pulled along as they walked up and down the lane in a wobbly snake-like pattern wishing one and all a Happy New Year. Neighbors broke out in song. Kate was handed a glass of sherry but, in the darkness and general commotion, could not tell from whence it came.

It was a chilly night made warm by a friendly community and the sherry. With no lighting in the lane except the dim glow from candles in windows, it was difficult to recognize others except by voice. Looking upward Kate marveled at the deep marine blue sky and the billions of stars set like diamonds into its velvet expanse.

She remembered how fascinated she was, as a child, by the wonder and beauty of the night sky when walking home from midnight mass with her parents. Suddenly she was brought back to the present by a voice close by.

"Let me pour you another drink," the voice from the semi-darkness suggested. She could not at first recognize who the speaker was and then remembered she had heard the voiced before.

"No, thank you, Mr. O'Toole."

"A bird never flew on one wing. Hold out your glass." She obliged. He poured.

"Thank you, and a Happy New Year to you," she said, before he had slipped away, becoming one of the silhouettes in the night.

Soon all the people were forming a loose circle. Some stood with their arms around their spouse, some held hands and others gently swayed to the sound of the song. A baritone voice began, and then all joined in singing "Auld Lang Syne." All glasses were raised at the words, "we take a drink for kindness sake."

"Happy New Year, and a long life filled with blessings," were Peg and Lil's wishes as they walked up to Kate when the singing was over.

"And to both of you and your families. Now tell me, how do I know to whom to return this glass?"

"Look underneath. What color do you see?"

"There's a tiny piece of yellow, I believe, taped to the bottom," Kate answered as she struggled to see in the dim light.

"Yellow belongs to Kathleen. I'm blue. Peg's purple. Don't

worry, just take it home with you tonight and return it to its owner tomorrow."

"Well, that solves that mystery. I spoke to Mr. O tonight who poured me a drink, but he was gone before I could thank him."

"How many drinks did you have, Kate?"

"Two." Just then Tara joined them.

"Kate here tells us she spoke to Old O tonight, and he poured her a drink!"

"I want whatever it is Kate's drinking," Tara laughed.

"You wouldn't catch him out wishing anyone a Happy New Year," Lil assured Kate. Kate knew it was Mr. O'Toole but decided not to the press the issue, believing O'Toole wanted it that way.

CHAPTER 6

Francis came across a position for a groom in the want ads, a position more suitable to his talents. After receiving directions to the farm in question, he set out for an interview.

He was pleasantly surprised by the beautiful layout of the farm. The owner and his wife, both excellent riders, needed a groom. The previous groom, who had been with them for a long time, had taken a bad fall from a horse. He could no longer exercise the horses or even brush them down. The farm owner invited Francis to ride with him. Francis enjoyed the ride immensely for he had not been on horseback since he had left his uncle's farm. The owner, Mr. Roundtree, gave his horse full reign, and Francis followed suit as they galloped along at great speed. The freedom of the open space, the gallop, the wind on his face was exhilarating to Francis and brought back memories of riding his horse on the open strand in Dublin in the early hours of the morning when the world seemed fresh and new.

On returning to the stable, Mr. Roundtree studied Francis' hands and smooth actions as he rubbed down the horses.

"What brought you to us?"

"I like working with horses."

"So you'd want this job?"

"That would depend on the salary you are offering."

Mr. Roundtree did not answer immediately but studied his well manicured nails as though the answer lay among his fingers.

"Where do you presently work?"

Francis mentioned the elite bookstore of his present employment.

"What did you do before coming to England?"

"I worked on my uncle's farm."

"You're obviously a skilled rider and can handle horses well."

"I began at age four."

Mr. Roundtree gave Francis the figure he was willing to offer. Francis wanted the job but hesitated.

"You drive a hard bargain," Mr. Roundtree said as he upped the salary.

"I believe I have a lot of experience with horses. Your horses would be in excellent hands if I accepted."

Mr. Roundtree upped the salary a notch more, saying he realized Francis was equal to the job and this was the best he could offer.

"Do you have family living in England?"

"No, my wife and son are living in Dublin."

"Does he ride?"

"Yes, as does his mother."

Mr. Roundtree smiled.

"Well, if you are trying to save money, you might like the digs we have here. It's not much, just a converted carriage house, one room, shower stall and bare minimum kitchen. I can let you have it rent free."

No rent. It's like getting an additional salary, Francis thought. He couldn't have felt happier if he had won the Irish Sweepstakes. Francis accepted the job.

The Roundtrees, who traveled quite frequently, needed their horses and those of their two sons, who were away at university, and the extra guest horses exercised, fed and cared for. Francis had a boss he liked, a job that he would look forward to doing every day, and he'd be finally able to save and give his family what he so very much wanted them to have.

It's so lonely in the lane without Francis, Kate lamented. With the holidays over and the cold of late January descending upon Dublin, people bundled up against the bone-chilling rain and did not tarry, but hurried on their way. Kate bought a sack of turf with the postal money order Francis sent, plus some staples: candles, flour, sugar, tea, potatoes, turnips, and carrots. The latter three she stored in the shed in the back yard. She set aside money for milk, cheese, eggs, and the like as needed. She also placed several shillings next to the gas meter.

She took sponge baths and bathed Eoin in front of the fire in the morning when she had a good blaze going. In late afternoon she refrained from replenishing the fire to save fuel, letting it turn to ash.

To keep Eoin's head, the only part of him exposed, warm during the night she had knitted him a little nightcap. The iron was permanently left on the hearth to keep it hot, so before putting him to bed for the night, she would run the hot iron over his night clothing and the crib sheets to warm them.

Like her neighbors, during the cold of winter, Kate retired for the night at an early hour. Before doing so, she would also run the hot iron over the sheets on her bed, then wrap the hot iron in a flannel shirt and place it under the covers at the end of the bed to keep her feet warm. With a candle and a book, she read in the quiet of the cottage with no sound save for the boisterous wind whipping the cottage and the rain playing patty cake against the windowpanes.

The Brothers Karamazov brought her into the Russia of an earlier period and showed her the complexities of emotions, passion, murder, and the secret depths of man's struggles within himself. While she enjoyed Dostoyevsky's novel, alone with a baby in these harsh winter months, she decided she needed something cheerful, or a good mystery novel to distract her from her lack of companionship. With Francis she could have borne all in good spirits, but without him the lane had become a wretchedly lonely place.

Morning came looking like night. Darkness and rain covered all. She shivered as her feet touched the icy cold floor. She had left her robe and slippers in her shared apartment, because she could not fit them into her suitcase that day, almost a year ago, when she made her way up the lane. Wanting to go back to the still warm bed, she knew that she could not do so. During the night, she had been called on to check the Dunne boy who had a fever, a condition she was able to reduce before leaving at three o'clock in the morning. Kate knew she had to check in on him again. There was just enough tap water to make a cup or two of tea. Putting the tea kettle on the flame, she brewed some tea. She needed to dash out and get some water as soon as the rain eased a bit. In her loneliness she told herself that hell was not hot but rather damp, cold, dark, and dreary.

Dampness covered everything outdoors and indoors. Only a very limited amount of clothing could be washed because there was no way of drying clothes. The baby's diapers, washed the previous day and still damp, were draped over the backs and seats of the kitchen chairs around the fireplace to dry, along with some of Kate's undergarments. This was the fifth day of rain, not a soft misty rain, but downpour after downpour of heavy drenching rain. It was as though this little rain-drenched island might become one with the sea.

In the dark weariness of her soul, she thought of Francis and what they had had and what they had lost. Her dark mood grew more intense as she struggled to light the fire with damp matches. Why had he not come to the cottage to tell her he was going to England? Was it too much to ask that he say goodbye to her? These questions bore into the core of her being, and in doing so ignited her anger. It was cowardly of him not to have done so. What kind of love has no forgiveness? He did not mention returning at a later date or where he planned to travel to, nor if he considered their marriage over. A piece of newspaper succumbed to the match's weak flame and ignited the remainder of the paper and kindling. A small victory achieved with greatly appreciated results.

A divorce could not be had in Ireland. A separation was the only relief for a marriage that did not hold. Would he see other women? Fall in love without being tricked into marriage? Begin a whole new life? It was downright shabby of him, more than shabby, it was damn cruel of him not to have enlightened her of his plans before leaving. As his lawfully married wife, he owed her that courtesy. Tears of frustration filled her eyes as she hastily dressed.

"Damn him, damn him to hell," she muttered through clenched teeth. She threw the tea, which had grown cold out onto the stones in the back yard. *Smile*, she demanded. *Pull yourself together*. After inhaling and exhaling several deep breaths, she closed the back door and walked over and glanced at her son.

"It's just you and me now, Eoin," she whispered over the sleeping child. "I'll be back in about twenty minutes. Sleep safely until then." Opening the door, she walked up the lane to check on the Dunne boy's health.

In March, Mr. O'Toole, who lived two cottages further up the lane from Kate, became quite sick. He refused to go to the hospital as recommended by his physician, declaring he wasn't ready to die yet.

People of Mr. O'Toole's generation believed that being taken to the hospital meant certain death. There was a great deal of truth to that since people resisted being seen by a doctor or entering a hospital until they were beyond medical intervention.

At the request of her neighbors, and though she felt there was little she could do for him except make him comfortable, Kate agreed to undertake his care. The women minded Eoin while Kate attended to Mr. O'Toole.

After several weeks of Kate's attention, Mr. O'Toole recovered from pneumonia. She informed her patient she would return to her accustomed activities within a few days but would check in on him occasionally.

Kate entered his cottage the next morning to make his breakfast, check his vital signs, and empty his commode, whereupon Mr. O'Toole said he had something important to discuss with her.

"Pull up a chair next to the bed, Kate." She did as requested and sat down.

"I have not been hasty in this decision I am about to convey to you." After a few moments of coughing, he continued. "I have made my will and the bulk of the money will go to young Eoin. I tell you this in confidence."

"Mr. O'Toole, I have attended to others who were injured or sick in the lane, all free of charge, and so, too, I do for you."

"I appreciate your generosity and care, and I thank you. However, it is Francis I'm thinking of in coming to this decision. Francis is like a son to me. What I couldn't do for Francis I can now do for his son. Don't deny me that."

I cannot deceive this old man. My child is not Francis' son and is not entitled to any money this man might have.

"Your little lad is my namesake. Yes, child, I wasn't baptized Old Man O'Toole or any variations of that. My given name is Eoin."

"As is my father's after whom I named my son."

"I didn't think you named him for me but what a grand coincidence it is."

Eoin O'Toole closed his eyes savoring this happy occurrence.

Oh God, here I go again. Am I ever going to be able to leave the past behind? Sheila as a friend and confident; Mary and Ned, for their better understanding of why Francis left Dublin; and now for an old man, past being ready to die, I must again uncover my shame.

"Francis and I were married, but Eoin is not Francis' child." And so Kate one more time revealed her past indiscretions from conception onwards. As she spoke he made no comment, but patiently and quietly listened. When she had finished, a brief silence followed, broken by a deep belly laugh by the patient, which soon caused a fit of coughing, more laughter and coughing. Kate was mortified, believing him insensitive to her plight. As the coughing and laughter continued, she stood up and announced, "You're a horrible old man. I told you the truth so as not to deceive you, and you laugh at my expense."

"No, Kate," he answered between coughs but no longer laughing, "It's not at you I laugh, old fool that I am. It's at myself."

Puzzled, she waited until his coughing has ceased and he was at rest.

"I too have a story to tell, one not too unlike yours. Sit, Kate."

He made an effort to raise himself up, and Kate propped another pillow behind his head. Now in a more comfortable position he was ready to speak.

"You remind me of her. She was a winsome lass, but alas, it wasn't to be."

After pausing to gather his thoughts, he began. "I haven't told this story to another living soul."

The O'Tooles lived on the avenue. The rear garden walls of the back gardens of these houses formed the solid high wall that led to the lane where Aoife Molloy and Francis Egan, Francis' father, lived. Aoife, the O'Toole brothers, Eoin and Dermot, Francis and other local children attended the nearby National School.

Eoin O'Toole was in love with Aoife from the moment he developed an interest in the opposite sex, and thought about marrying her long before boys of his age thought that far ahead. In their teens, they spent summers bicycling, swimming, and attending local dances, never as a twosome but in groups as was the custom.

Dermot, Eoin's younger brother by five years, had done well in university, married well and became what his father referred to as 'established.' Eoin, alas, was a disappointment to their father, who believed a young man had no right to encourage a serious friendship with a girl until he was settled in a career.

Eoin's friendship with Aoife was the most important happening in his young life. They walked together holding hands when not in the immediate neighborhood. Aoife was the fiber of his daydreams.

All the negative aspects of women as spoken of by the Christian Bothers, who wished to deter their students from sexual encounters, held no weight for him. Besides, he reasoned, if young women were the 'putrid vessels' the brothers spoke of, why were mothers honored? Were they not once young women, too? It was then that he realized the trip down the aisle was the dividing line. Once it was crossed all was well. And so his daydreams expanded as he walked down the aisle with Aoife, a vision in a pretty dress, carrying a bouquet of flowers.

His daydreams were reinforced by every smile and greeting from Aoife and by the feel of her hand in his. When in groups, they went alone to pick firewood for the campfire, and on the strand slowed their steps to distance themselves from the others. Eoin pursued Aoife until he entered university.

The year he was to graduate, he discovered Aoife and Francis Egan, a good-looking, honorable man, had been keeping company and became engaged to marry. Francis Egan was employed and ready to settle down.

In temporary insanity, Eoin found himself hating Francis and furious with his father who, in bestowing upon him an education, had separated him from Aoife. In anger he left the country, breaking his mother's heart and displaying gross ingratitude to his father. During his first year or more of self-imposed exile, he wandered from country to country across the continent and then settled in England.

"I had a good paying government position."

"Not being English, how did you get a position with the British government?" Kate intruded.

"Ireland had not yet become a free state. Ireland under English rule made me a British subject."

Eoin O'Toole had several promotions over his years in England and was earning a vast amount of money that he could not have made in Ireland. With nobody to spend it on, he saved his money. About a dozen years later, he returned to Ireland where he invested his money in property and land. Poverty was rampant in Ireland at that time, but he believed Ireland would rise out of her slave mentality, once free, and would prosper. Alas, it was decades before that happened. The civil war followed independence as a result of England carving out the six northern counties for herself. Also, Ireland had been under domination of a superior force for so long, her people were as free as the beggars roaming the street. There were no jobs, no money in the treasury. Yes, Ireland was free, but dire poverty remained.

"I could have bought Aoife a beautiful house in an upper class neighborhood but Aoife had happily settled down in the lane. I purposely met her as she shopped for groceries. She was as lovely as ever except the joy that had been so much a part of her had left. Oh, she was still in love with Francis. The problem, I learned, was that they were already ten years married and without child. Both of them very much wanted children.

After speaking with her over time, I offered a suggestion, which at first she out and out rejected. Months later, desperate to have a child, she consented. Regardless of the outcome, success or failure, we agreed, we would attempt it to fulfill her wish, just once. As planned, we boarded a train to Killiney in mid-morning, rented a room, and we were back home by mid-afternoon. Aoife got pregnant and gave birth to a son. I had no claim on the child. As little Francis grew, he called another man 'daddy.' A few years later I moved into the lane in order to be able to see Francis."

"That's so sad. So that's why you said, 'what I couldn't do for Francis I can now do for his son.' Does Francis know?"

"No, Kate. How could I tell him that he was the result of the sexual encounter I had with his mother, unknown to his father?"

"You couldn't share in their joy?"

"Yes, Kate, I did. I gave the woman I loved the gift she wanted most. Her happiness was my greatest joy."

"Why didn't you marry another after Aoife married another man?"

"That would have been unfair to another for I never stopped loving Aoife."

"I'm so sorry."

"Why, Kate?"

"I have disappointed you. You thought my son was your grandson!"

"I still wish to set up a trust for little Eoin with you as the trustee."

"Even though you don't know who Eoin's father is?"

"I know his mother."

"You're a remarkable man, Eoin O'Toole."

"We've both paid dearly for no other crime than having loved passionately."

Bending down, Kate kissed him on the cheek, and left.

CHAPTER 7

Not only did Harry Browne see himself as a self-made man, he also saw himself as the creator of his own good fortune. He, a poor boy from the tenements, had accomplished his dream—marrying into inherited wealth.

He and his young bride had a lavish wedding, written up in the society columns, and a honeymoon touring France in a BMW, a wedding gift to the young couple from the bride's father, Brian Fitzgerald.

His wife Kit, an only child, was a bit spoiled, he believed, but that would not be a problem to him, a man whom all his friends agreed had a way with women. Kit, like most women, loved him.

Nineteen-year-old Kit was a petite girl with what Harry considered a nice figure, though a bit on the chubby side. His plan was to take care of her tendency towards extra poundage after they had a baby. In Harry's opinion she was not too bright, but was someone he could convince to see things his way.

All Brian Fitzgerald, Kit, the trainer, and farm workers spoke of were horses. It was food and drink to them. Newborn foals brought great excitement. When one of their own horses or those they boarded and trained had won a race, they cheered and celebrated as though, as Harry had commented, "they had won the world soccer cup."

Since Harry had no home to bring his bride, it was agreed they would live at the Fitzgerald's. In these idyllic surroundings, Harry, who normally avoided work as much as possible, and now having absolutely nothing to do, was bored. Fitzgerald presided over a farm run by people who loved, understood, and cared for horses as Fitzgerald himself did. Harry, although skittish around horses, believed he, the son-in-law, should have been given a position of authority on the farm. But it was not forthcoming. He brooded.

Now two years into the marriage and with no heir, Brian Fitzgerald had a way of indirectly asking why Harry had not yet sired a grandson. He irked the young husband and compounded his misery until Harry grew to hate the farm and wanted to leave it and live elsewhere. He had, however, no funding of his own. All his needs were taken care of through the generosity of his wife. Not only that, but he soon learned that as the husband of the much loved Kit, he had to stay put. This was the family home. Whether in paradise or hell, he was a prisoner.

One raining, thundering night when Harry was trying to have his wife conceive, a loud knocking was heard on their bedroom door, followed by Brian Fitzgerald's voice, "I need you, Kit. Gracie's foal is coming ahead of time, and the men won't be back from Suffix Downs until the day after tomorrow."

Kit immediately slid out from under Harry and into her robe, before opening the door.

"Come, honey, we'll do it together. It's just the two of us now."

Kit left with her father without looking back into the room where Harry lay on the bed in frustration and anger. *Those bloody horses!* Harry thought. *I too am just a stud. I'm a liability! They'd sell me off if they could. I can produce! I have produced! I'm so damn productive, kids who weren't wanted came. It's the Fitzgerald family line that's defective.*

Harry punched the pillow. He was too aggravated to sleep. As his anger weakened, he wondered what had happened to that girl who said she was a nurse. Some nurse! She didn't know enough to protect herself. She was a classy looking girl but not too bright. There were four of them sharing a tiny flat in a dump of a neighborhood. No family money there.

She never did pick up the money I left with the bartender in the Mouse that Roared, which means she must have kept the baby. Was it a girl or a boy? What would Fitzgerald think if he knew? What was her name? She married Francis Egan, but I heard he left her and took off for England. So she was left to raise the kid in poverty. Maybe I could relieve her of that responsibility. How old would it be? He mentally calculated, *somewhere between one and two years old.*

Do Kit and Fitzgerald want a child enough to accept a child of mine rather than one from their bloodline? If Kit and I had a child together, it would be me who sired it. Well, this stallion has already procreated. I could persuade Kit without much difficulty to accept a child of mine, but getting her father to accept a bastard as his heir may be insurmountable. Well, maybe not. If Kit wants the child, I feel confident; her father will cave into his daughter's desire.

Harry decided to locate the mother and offer her a lump sum

of money for the child. She's young, very attractive, and can have other children. Suddenly Harry's mood was brighter, and his brain was a whirlwind of activity. He hoped the girl had a boy. A boy might more easily sway Fitzgerald than a girl.

Harry put on his trousers, a shirt, and boots, and walked toward the horse stalls. The mare was in trouble. It was going to be a difficult delivery.

"We need to get inside of her," Fitzgerald said. Kit now standing behind the mare took off her robe and threw it over the stall gate. Kit put her hand into the horse. Tense moments followed.

"I can't find one of her legs."

"Keep trying, honey," he encouraged her. "If anyone can do it, it is you." Seeing a look of concern cloud Kit's face, he asked, "What is it?"

"One leg seems bent in a partial kneeling position."

Fitzgerald did not instruct her further. He had confidence in Kit's abilities and remained silent to allow her to concentrate. The silence seemed to prolong the time, and time was of an essence as Kit delicately maneuvered the errant leg into position.

Moments later she pulled out her arm, and in her fist were skinny legs, soon followed by the rest of the animal, which slid out effortlessly. The foal struggled to stand, gained its balance walked a few step until it was side by side with its mother.

Harry, who had been standing in the shadows, unnoticed by father and daughter, was amazed by his wife's abilities and calmness throughout this whole ordeal. He looked at Kit's face lit up in joy and at her handkerchief thin white nightgown now covered in blood. Yet, regardless of this utter mess, she looked beautiful. For the first time since he had known her, he could truly say, 'I love you, Kit Fitzgerald.'

"You've done a great job, honey. Gracie, our new mother, is most thankful as am I." And in saying this, he hugged his daughter who wrapped her blood-stained hands around her father. When they released their hold on each other, Brian's expensive robe was blood stained. Yet, to Harry's amazement, none of this bothered either of them. Harry had never seen two people so comfortably happy. Horses were their livelihood, their area of expertise and their passion. It was bred in their bones.

"Wish I, too, could have a baby," she told her father.

"You will, honey. Just give it time."

"Mom died when my baby brother was born, and you lost both of them. More than anything I want to give you a grandson."

"And you will. Don't despair. It will happen in God's own time."

"I've heard of girls going to England to have abortions, and here am I desperately wanting a baby and not having one. It doesn't seem fair."

Harry had never heard his wife speak like this before. His reasons for wanting her to conceive was not for his wife, who never complained to him, but to appease her father and wipe the smug smirks from the trainers' and farm workers' faces. This was a breeding farm, and he failed to breed. He quickly left the stall to avoid being noticed and hid in the shadows outside as Kit and his father-in-law emerged. With his arm around his daughter, they walked to the main house, greatly satisfied with the night's work.

"Yes," Harry thought, "I'll find my child for you."

Kate, responding to the knock on the door, opened it. The last person on earth she expected to see was standing there, smiling. *Why?* she thought.

"You're looking well, Kate, but then you were always a head turner."

"What brings you here? How did you know where I lived?" she asked in surprise.

"Whoa, there girl. Don't I get a hello? You're staying in Egan's cottage made finding you easy. Ah, then there's the why I'm here," he said as he pushed passed her into the cottage. Seeing a crib across the room, he headed in that direction. The manner in which the child was dressed did not indicate if it were a girl or boy. And Harry needed to know.

"So this is our child?"

"No, my child. You didn't want it."

"Whose name did you put down on the birth certificate as the father?"

"Francis Egan."

"That's a lie. He isn't the father."

"He's my husband. This is my child."

"He hasn't been around lately, I heard. Actually he left before the child was born, and it's now almost two years old. Correct me if I'm wrong?"

He waited.

She did not respond.

Harry, who had been silently inspecting the room in which he stood, continued.

"Yes, I know I did you a wrong. I left you when you were pregnant, but then, didn't Francis do likewise. Oh, yes, our reasons were different, but our actions were the same. You're a very attractive young woman, Kate. You can do better than wait around for Egan to return."

Good grief, I think Harry may be proposing. Surely he does not believe we could pick up the pieces and go on from where the relationship ended? Yet, she was flattered, then annoyed with herself for being so, and reminded herself that Harry has no principles, no honor, but has an overabundance of selfishness.

"I could provide the child with every advantage." Realizing he still does not know if it's male or female, he asked, "What's its name?"

"He has all the advantages in life he needs, Harry."

A boy! Great ! Harry thought.

I wish he'd say whatever he's trying to say, she thought.

"Harry, what exactly is the reason for your visit?"

"You don't understand, Kate. I married a girl, an only child, whose father owns the biggest stud farm in Kildare. They're filthy rich. As my son, and the owner's grandson, he'll not want for anything. Not only that, but I'm willing to give you a sizeable sum of money."

"My son?" she asked in horror. "Your wife wants my son?"

"She doesn't know about this child. She just wants a child, and I aim to get her one."

"Your ideas and actions are insane."

"Nobody likes living in poverty, Kate. If you don't want the money, I can purchase you a house of your choosing in Booterstown, Blackrock, or any place you'd fancy."

"My son isn't for sale. Get out of my cottage!" she answered anger rising in her voice.

"You'll regret this. The next person you'll have to speak with will be my lawyer's solicitor. We can do this nicely or it can be nasty. You'll lose the child either way, so think it over."

"You wanted him aborted!"

"That's your word against mine. You surely don't think my friend the bartender would side with you! And when it comes out that you married Egan so as to pass the child off as his, what do you think that will do to your reputation or credibility?"

Turning to the crib where the child stood looking at two adults barter, Harry said,

"I can take him out of this miserable place now," and he stretched his arm around the child's waist, about to pick him up.

The child, who had been entertained by this stranger, became frightened and began to cry.

Kate grabbed the hot iron from the fireplace. Her intent was to touch his back gently with the hot iron. As soon as he felt the heat of the iron, he would jump, releasing Eoin. Instead, Harry abruptly turned around while striking out his hand, hitting it against the flat of the iron. Immediately a scream burst forth from Harry. As his face contorted, he forced himself to inhale gathering the pain and dragging it down inside of him, but not before the frightened child gave out a loud sorrowful cry. Kate hastened towards her son, picked him up and soothed his fears.

"You bloody bitch," Harry said in a low menacing voice. "You dirty tramp. You tried to kill me!"

Recovering from the shock of what had happened, she told him,

"If I wanted a corpse in my cottage, I would have hit you on the head with the iron."

Harry, in pain, held the wrist of his burnt hand, his face drained of color.

"Where is the cold water, damn it?"

"I'm sorry. There is no cold water here. You'll have to go down the lane to the water tap you passed on your way here."

She opened the door. As he left, through clenched teeth, he spat out the words, "You'll pay for this, you damn bitch. My lawyer will know you deliberately burnt me and tried to kill me."

"It's your words against mine, Harry. There are no witnesses."

Harry rushed down to the tap and put his hand under the flow of water, wetting his shoes, the front of his trousers, and his coat sleeves. After a few minutes he was gone.

Kate, shaken from the ordeal, put the child in the crib, pulled over a chair and sat down beside the crib. Her heart was pounding, her legs felt like jelly, and her mind was disorganized. *Have some tea,* she advised herself. In order to do so, she will need to fetch water, but her body refused to move.

After a brief time, she forced herself to get up. Going to the crib, she picked Eoin up, holding him closely to her breast. *Could I lose him? No, don't think the worst possible outcome,* she chided herself. *Pull yourself together.*

With the child in her arms, she left the cottage and walked up to O'Toole's cottage where she knocked on the door.

"Come in," a voice from within called to her.

"Kate," O'Toole smiled from his armchair by the fire, and then his expression quickly turned serious. "What is the matter, Kate? You're as white as a ghost, lass. Are you sick?"

Kate shook her head.

"Is it the boy?" Again she shook her head.

Breathlessly, she told O'Toole of her unexpected visitor, the purpose of his visit, and what took place in her cottage. O'Toole listened silently and remained quiet for several moments after she had finished.

"Put the boy down on my lap, and make us some tea. There's a tin of biscuits waiting to be opened on the shelf over the stove."

"I don't think I can eat anything," Kate replied as she set about making the tea.

"You haven't seen anything as delicious as these," he told her. "They're the kind you don't have to have an appetite to eat. One look into the assortment in that box will do it."

Despite her anguish, Kate smiled.

"I'll take a plain one for Eoin," she told O'Toole and, opening the box, she saw the richness of its contents. "Oh, nothing plain here, Mr. O'Toole" she smiled. "Well, Eoin you're going to love this one with the hard icing on it," and she handed the biscuit to the child, who smiled and said, "Tank you."

"You're the only one in the lane who knows about Eoin's true parentage. Although if Harry Browne gets a lawyer, it will most likely make all the newspapers, and all will know."

As she set the cups and saucers on the small bench next to

O'Toole's armchair, and poured the tea, he spoke. "You'll need a good lawyer, Kate."

"I don't know the first thing about engaging a lawyer," she answered as she took Eoin from O'Toole to enable him to have his tea. Eoin on her lap.

"Leave that to me. We're not going to let young Eoin go off to any stud farm. We'll fight."

Eoin insisted on grabbing for his mother's teacup. Since Mr. O'Toole had just two teacups, Kate rose with the child in her arms, walked to the shelf and took an eggcup off it. Then she poured in milk, added a few teaspoons of tea, a pinch of sugar, and sitting down, handed it to the child, who happily drank.

"You had said Francis sends you a small amount of money monthly. Do you have receipts?"

"No, but I've been depositing the money he sends into a separate bank account since I returned to work a year ago. Before that time I cashed the money orders at the post office and used them for our needs."

"May I ask what name is on this account?"

"Francis and Kate Egan."

"Ah, good."

"In what way?"

"It shows he has sent money towards the support of you and the child." He paused to drink some tea then continued. "You've mentioned the effects on the people of the lane should this become public. It is my belief that Browne and his in-laws would have many more problems with this kind of publicity. Browne wants the child, so we'll assume his wife and he cannot conceive a child of their own. His father-in-law, a rich man used to having things his way, cannot be happy accepting Browne's child by a woman other than his daughter as his grandchild. I doubt very much if the stud farm owner's pride could withstand all his friends, workers, and business associates knowing that his grandson was not of his bloodline, but a child of his son-in-law, born to a woman he got pregnant and of whom he had no intention of marrying."

"Mr. O'Toole, you give me hope."

"What they will want, Kate, above all, is for this case *not* to go to court. Believing you can't hire an attorney, and knowing they can't bribe you to give up the child, they feel safe in threatening you with a court case. You don't have a telephone. Therefore, if Browne does engage a lawyer, you can expect to have a visit from the lawyer's solicitor. When or if he arrives, do not discuss any of this with him. Instead, you and young Eoin should bring him here, and here we'll speak with him."

"I will. Do you know of a lawyer who will take this case should we need one?" Kate asked as she washed the teacups, saucers and spoons.

"I'll go tomorrow and speak with my brother and see about enlisting the services of Gilmartin, Rowan and O'Toole.

"Is your brother a lawyer?"

"No, Kate. He's a judge.

"A judge?"

"Yes. His son is a lawyer, with the just mentioned firm, which is why when the solicitor arrives, you will introduce me as Eoin, no surname."

"What if he asks for your full name?"

"Don't worry about that. Just bring him here. I will take care of the rest." As she and the child were about to leave, O'Toole called to her, "Kate, don't breathe a word of this to anyone. I don't make my family or private affairs known to others."

"I won't tell a soul."

As Eoin O'Toole had predicted, several days later, Harry Browne's lawyer had sent his solicitor to call on Kate. On hearing a knock on the door, instead of the customary words, 'come in,' Kate interrupted Eoin's climb on the chair to reach the table where the freshly baked soda bread lay on a rack to cool, and picked him up before she opened the door.

"Mrs. Egan?"

"Yes."

"I'm George Connelly for the law firm of Bailey, Duff and Harris." Kate removed her coat from the back of the door, and casting it over Eoin's and her own head against the heavy rainfall, moved forward closing the door behind her.

"Come with me," she said simply.

"Do you not live in that cottage?" he asked turning around to point back at the Egan cottage, for Kate walked ahead without breaking her stride.

"Yes, but we can't discuss this matter there." He obediently followed.

"I have an umbrella," he said, and catching up with her, held it over her and the child's head. *Who is in her cottage,* he wondered, *whose presence she doesn't want known? Is it a boy friend? This might alter the case, but I don't have the authority to demand entrance. I will report it.*

Kate knocked on O'Toole's door. On hearing his voice call out,

Kate entered, followed by George Connelly. O'Toole with his back to them lowered the bellows he has been using on the fire, sending sparks jumping up the chimney. As he turned around, Kate introduced the two men stating, "Eoin, this is Mr. Connelly from the firm of Bailey, Duff and Harris."

"Sit you both down," O'Toole offered. "Now Mr. Connelly, what brings you here?"

George Connelly gave his reasons, which were pretty much as Harry Browne had stated them only in a more gracious manner. After he had finished, he sat in much discomfort and waited for a response from either O'Toole or Kate. Since it was a cold, raw, rainy day, Connelly had dressed warmly, too warmly for this small room with its blazing hot fire. O'Toole, who normally was most particular about such things, had neglected to empty his chamber pot this morning. The one window in the room was shut tight against the cold and rain. Mr. Connelly began to perspire profusely in this mixture of dampness and heat.

"Would you like a nice hot cup of tea, Mr. Connelly?" O'Toole asked.

"No, thank you, sir."

"Well, now, you have set your purpose clearly, and I will be equally clear. We intend to engage a lawyer and fight this case, and, I believe, we'll win."

"Have you any idea how costly hiring a lawyer can be?"

"Yes, indeed I do," he answered shaking his head. "I have engaged the law firm of Gilmartin, Rowan and O'Toole."

"Mr . . . eh I don't believe you mentioned your surname?"

"I'm known as Eoin. You may call me Eoin. As you were saying?"

"Gilmartin, Rowan, and O'Toole are tops in this business. They . . ."

"Yes, I know, Mr. Connelly. That is why we've engaged them. They have agreed we have an excellent case. Mr. Browne convinced this young woman that he loved her and planned to marry her. After she became pregnant with his child, he abandoned her in that condition. Now, after absolutely no contact with her for the past three years, he finds his wife and he cannot conceive a child, and wants to claim the child he tried to get this woman to abort. This case will produce a great deal of publicity. Can Mr. Browne's and his wife's marriage survive it? And more importantly, what will this kind of publicity do to Mr. Fitzgerald, owner of the most prestigious stud farm in Kildare? He will, no doubt, do all in his power to quench this case; thus, the father-in-law of your own client will also be working against you and your law firm. You have opened Pandora's box. Mr. Connelly, convey this to the lawyer who will represent Mr. Browne. Tell him, also, in compensation, we will agree to a sum of money, the amount yet to be determined, and to be given to the local orphanage. This money is to be used to help children as they come of age to leave the orphanage, and to finance their start in the outside world."

Connelly was beginning to feel ill. The heat was overpowering as was the odor in the room.

"Do take off your coat, Mr. Connelly," Kate urged, for she felt sorry for his distress.

"Is it giving comfort to the enemy you are, Kate?" O'Toole jokingly questioned her.

Connelly smiled wanly, and refused her offer. He wanted very much to leave, but knew he had to stay a while longer.

"Sir, why would you expect a donation to be made on your behalf by a client of ours?"

"You have grieved this young woman and tried to take her child from her. Since she is a kind-hearted woman, a donation to such a worthy cause, I feel, will alleviate the damage done to her by your client, Mr. Browne."

Connelly rose. He had to leave before he embarrassed himself by being sick.

"I will see what can be done," he answered.

"We must have an answer within a week," O'Toole told him.

"Have we met before? You look familiar. I seem to recognize you from someplace?"

"That's hardly likely, Mr. Connelly. We don't move in the same circles, and I can assure you, I've never met you prior to this meeting." A brief silence followed.

"I can see myself out, thank you." Connelly said, as Kate rose to walk him to the door. The rain had stopped, but Connelly was soaked inside and out from perspiration and rain. He took a deep breath once he had closed the door behind him, then he walked briskly down the lane.

As the door closed behind Connelly, O'Toole laughed.

"I'm sorry, Kate, that you had to breathe in this odor. Quickly take yourself and the boy out and don't come back until I've emptied the chamber pot and aired this place out."

"You did this on purpose? That poor man sweated, and he could hardly breathe."

"All part of the plan. I figured he would not come yesterday, that would have been too soon. He might come today, and if he didn't,

I would have wasted my turf and kindling. Worse than that, each day I would have had to keep the chamber pot in the cottage until he came. I can now let the fire die down a bit and empty the pot."

"You're a wicked man, Eoin O'Toole."

"When need be, Kate, when need be. Now leave, Kate, and let me do what I have to do."

"Thank you. You're also a very kind man."

"Kate!"

"Yes, Mr. O'Toole."

"Buy a decent coat, and get rid of the old rain coat you've been wearing since you arrived in the lane."

"Yes, sir, in due time," she laughed, and taking the child, Kate returned to her cottage.

When Kate arrived back at the cottage, she noticed a letter had been dropped into the mail slot. Opening it she read Sheila's letter. In a fortnight's time, Sheila would be leaving England for Australia where she had secured a job. She wanted Kate and Eoin to come to England and sail with her to Australia. Sheila enthused about how wonderful living in Australia would be, how it would be a new start for Kate and Eoin, and how much in need of nurses was Sydney.

That night Kate wrote to Sheila telling her of Browne's visit, and the solicitor's visit, and how wonderfully Eoin O'Toole handled the whole matter. Now they awaited the outcome. She also mentioned that she didn't want to take Eoin's heritage away. Her son was Irish. Yes, she knew he might grow up and leave Ireland, but that would be his decision, not one she had made for him. Then there was Francis. He had never given her his address, but he did send money monthly from someplace in England.

Sheila wrote back immediately. She thought Kate was making a big mistake. Eoin would probably emigrate after he finished school in Ireland. Then she'd be alone with nothing but missed opportunities. Sheila also gave Kate the benefit of her thoughts on Francis, who she believed was keeping Kate dangling from a string while he was living it up in England, and suggested that the reason he never gave Kate his address was he didn't want his present girlfriend to know about her.

There may be some truth to what Sheila believed, Kate thought, but she was determined to have Eoin grow up in Ireland. Perhaps Francis has no plans to come home. If this is so, why would he send money each month? That doesn't suffice for his absence. She desperately wanted to hear from Francis and to know what his plans were and if they included her and Eoin. She would wait seven years before she would consider their marriage ended. In the meantime, she had a son and a part-time nursing job, and was grateful for both. She also had the cottage and the best possible neighbors living in the lane. She and Eoin also had good friends in Ned and Mary with whom they spent all holidays. They loved Eoin, and expressed a great desire to take care of him during summer vacation when he was old enough to attend school and she could work full time. There was also O'Toole, who saw Eoin as his grandson. O'Toole was a good friend to her, and she loved the dear old man. Yes, Eoin was being well cared for among generous, loving people.

More than three months had passed since Harry had visited the law firm. He was impatient with the delays. His constant telephone calls to the office never permitted him the opportunity to speak with any of the lawyers, only the receptionist or a solicitor. The solicitors, he felt, kept putting off with the same noncommittal language. 'We're working on it, Mr. Browne. These things take time and cannot be rushed, Mr. Browne,' and 'We pride ourselves on doing a thorough job, and getting the desired results for our clients.'

Now, he sat down for dinner at the Fitzgerald's on Sunday evening. Just before dessert was served, Brian Fitzgerald, sniffing his brandy, turned to Harry and said, "I need an explanation from you!"

"An explanation?" Harry, caught off guard, sputtered.

"I had a conversation with Mr. Duff of Harris, Bailey, and Duff law firm. He told me you've lost interest in producing a child the manly way, and are seeking to 'buy' a baby!"

An uncomfortable silence occurred, whereupon the horse trainer rose and said, "I'll be calling it a night. Goodnight to all," and with a head movement that told the jockey he should do likewise, they both left the room just as Brian had expected they would.

"What do you know of this, Kit?"

"Harry said since we were having so much trouble having a baby, he would get me a baby from a woman he knew of who was unmarried and had a baby about two and a half years old. We wouldn't be buying a child! This woman and child were living in great poverty, and we would be doing this unfortunate woman a favor by giving the baby a good home, and giving her a lump sum of money to help her get her life back in order."

"Is that the full extent of what he told you of his plan?"

"Yes. Harry also said it was a beautiful baby boy, and as soon as we knew for sure we could get this baby, we were going to tell you about our good news. I thought you'd be happy."

"Let me fill you in on a few details that he omitted. The woman in question was a girlfriend of Harry's whom he got pregnant and deserted. She married after Harry left her, and her husband is working in England. This woman, whom Harry had told to get an abortion, does not now, nor ever did wish to give up her child."

Kit, horrified by what she was told about Harry, stood to leave the table, but her father gently covered her hand with his, and she lowered herself back into the chair.

"As painful as it is for you, my dear, you need to know the details and the character of the man you married."

"I shall leave and the two of you can talk this over," Harry offered, as he rose from the chair.

"Sit down. You're not going anywhere at the moment."

"Kate, the mother of this child, is employed. Her husband and she own the cottage she and the child live in. When Mr. Connelly, the solicitor, paid her a call, she told him she had no intention of giving up her son, she had engaged a lawyer, and would fight the case. After what Harry told Connelly, and after Connelly's evaluation of the woman, he investigated further and found she did indeed have a lawyer, one of the best, from the law firm of Gilmartin, Rowan, and O'Toole, who believe she has a good case. The ugly publicity will smell worse than a fresh cartload of manure if this goes to court."

"She's bluffing. Neither she or Francis Egan have any money," Harry interjected.

Ignoring Harry's outburst, Brian Fitzgerald continued.

"After checking into the woman's background, the solicitor also discovered she was living where she lived from choice. Her father, now deceased, was a well-known dental surgeon who left a lucrative practice in Dublin, and settled in a small town in Wexford shortly after his daughter was born. One son has taken over the father's practice; the other son is a university professor married to another professor. This young mother comes into a nice sum of money when she turns twenty-five years old."

Harry was dumbfounded. After the initial shock, he became angry. *That deceitful whore made me think she was a poor working girl. I should have asked about her background. But damn it, she acted like she was destitute. Stupid like a fox was she.*

"Ah yes, nothing shabby about this young woman," Brian continued." Also, in order to drop the case, a sum of money, the amount to be decided on by her, must be donated to a local orphanage."

Kit sobbed.

"In time, love, you'll realize you're well rid of him."

"Pack your belongings, Harry. Pack only your personal belongings, and be out of this house before midnight. If you take as much as a paperclip that's not yours, I'll have you arrested. I've taken the liberty of closing all bank accounts, clothing shop accounts, and anything else with your name on it. My lawyer will let you know the sum of money to be donated to the orphanage, which you will pay over a set period of time."

Harry, who wished to leave earlier, could now hardly rise from the chair.

Slowly he arose and walked out of the room, glancing back just briefly to get Kit's reaction. Kit sat with her head in her hands, oblivious to his leaving.

Harry could hardly believe what he had heard. *Kate had an inheritance*! Harry heard the words repeat themselves in his head. *Money! And there wouldn't have been a damn father-in-law to make life difficult for him. How could he have so badly misjudged that affair? And to think he could have had it all!*

I thank my lucky stars, Harry sighed, *that I had the foresight to open up a bank account in my own name outside of Dublin where I've been depositing all the 'pocket money, and 'hand-outs' from the Fitzgeralds', plus the money I had been diverting from Kit's and my joint account. I now have plenty of well-tailored clothes, the finest shoes, shirts and accessories to become acquainted with a better class of ladies. Now, where should I go from here?*

Kate was happy that this nightmare turned out to be just a fairy tale. The case was won in her favor, and she was delighted that the children leaving the orphanage would benefit from what had happened. Yet, lingering in the back of her mind was the unpleasant feeling that Harry Browne would, at some point in the future, enter her life again.

CHAPTER 8

The summer before Eoin's fourth birthday, Kate decided to take him by train to the small town where she had grown up. Excited by the sight of the huge steam engine, which bellowed dark misty clouds onto the platform, and intermittently hissed steam, the boy was held spellbound.

"A live dragon," Kate laughed, as she boarded the train after Eoin who took a window seat. As her son watched the activity on the platform, Kate remembered her train rides to and from secondary school with friends.

As the train pulled into yet another well-maintained station on its way south, Eoin eagerly asked, "Is this it?"

"No, Eoin."

As they ate sandwiches Kate had prepared, she told the eager child, "Seven train stops from this stop, we will arrive at our destination." The boy held up seven fingers and at each stop he diligently counted each stop until they finally came to Gory.

"Yes, Eoin this is it," Kate answered, as she looked out at the station, the last and the first part of what she saw of her hometown when leaving from and returning to boarding school. "See, there is its name displayed in flowers."

"Do you think it won this year's award for most beautiful station?" he asked, remembering that she had told him that each station's name was beautifully displayed in colorful plants and flowers and decorated with sea shells, as each station competed for the award as 'most beautifully displayed and maintained railway station.'

"We'll have to ask the stationmaster," she smiled at his eagerness. Not wanting to concern her young son with her own apprehensions about going home again, she concentrated on his needs. They alighted from the train with their small suitcase in tow, the suitcase she carried when she first entered the lane nearly five years earlier. So much had happened since that day when she carried Eoin in her womb, not knowing what the future held for either her or for the child. Now, on returning to her hometown, she felt as vulnerable as she did that first day in the lane.

What kind of reception would she receive from her mother and brothers? More importantly, how would they receive her son, a child whose existence they were as yet unaware of?

"There's the stationmaster, Mr. Tierney, up ahead." They moved towards the uniformed gray-haired man with his whistle at the ready. Standing before him, Eoin spoke.

"Sir, did your station win the beautiful flower award this year?" A smile of pride immediately rose across the man's face.

"Yes, we did. You see, it's not my station exclusively. A lot of people make and help keep this station beautiful. Third year in a row we won! Would you like to see the award ribbon?"

"Yes," the little boy happily responded.

Kate was glad that Eoin's first moments in her hometown began with a good impression. She hoped that their stay here would continue in like manner.

Mr. Tierney beckoned them to follow him into the front office. Pointing to a row of large blue ribbons with round white centers and the words "1st Prize" written on them, he said, "These ribbons speak for themselves." On a less prominent wall were smaller ribbons that denoted second place and honorable-mention ribbons. "Here is a photograph of the people who work hard to keep up appearances." Eoin had no interest in the smiling people in the photograph.

"So, young man, you like our station display?"

"Yes, sir. It is very beautiful."

"Is this your mother here?" he asked the child while looking at Kate, and before the boy could answer, the stationmaster said, "Kate McCormack, as I live and breathe! Home on holidays, is it?"

"Yes, Mr. Tierney, and this is my son Eoin."

"And a fine young man he is indeed." Turning to the boy, the stationmaster held out his hand and shook the child's hand. "I knew your grandfather well. If you grow up to be half the man he was, you'll do your mother proud. Your grandfather was one of the finest men I ever set eyes on. And you, young man, have the honor of carrying his name. Don't ever dishonor that trust."

Noticing a couple of passengers standing by waiting to have a word with him, Mr. Tierney ended the interlude by saying, "It's good to see you home again, Kate, and to have met this young man of yours."

"Thank you, Mr. Tierney," she answered as she and Eoin left the building.

Outside the station she engaged a sidecar to take them to her mother's house. The driver she remembered as a rather slothful boy of yesteryear. Sitting on his sidecar under the shade of a huge old chestnut tree, he gave the impression they were disturbing his peaceful rest. He did not seem to recognize her. She gave him the address.

"McCormack's place?" he said in recognition. She nodded.

Riding through town, it appeared as though it had been suspended in time, oblivious to the world outside. The driver did not hurry the horse which trotted along at its own slow pace, while Kate gave Eoin a brief history of the places they passed. As they drove past Nancy's house, Kate offered a silent prayer for her.

Have I given too much information to a child so young, she wondered as he gazed at this place, fresh and new to his eyes? She had taken him to the library from the time he first began to learn nursery rhymes. She read to him, and he soon read to her from his books after supper each night as the written word became familiar to him. He bade her goodnight each evening knowing that his bedtime was his mother's time to enjoy reading from her books. When they picked up the morning newspaper, he would try to read the headlines and would question the photographs, wishing to know who the people were, why people walked with banners, and what was written on them. Kate found herself explaining strikes, unions, protests, buildings, politicians, soccer players, actor, plays being shown and anything he wished to know about as she read the newspaper.

"Look, Momma, at the boys playing soccer on the road," Eoin said with great excitement, as Kate inwardly regretted the lack of children in the lane. The teenage boys occasionally kicked a ball with him, but there were none his age to play with. In autumn he will begin school, Kate thought, and the problem of not having children of his own age with whom to interact will be resolved.

There was no time to think further on the matter as her childhood home had come into view. "We're here," she said as she brushed Eoin's hair in place with her gloved hand, gloves she had not worn since the day she arrived in the lane.

The slow moving horse moved slower and came to a stop in front of the house.

"Momma, this is a beautiful house. It has lots and lots of pretty flowers in the garden. Would you not like to live here?"

"Your grandfather planted those roses and all the plants when I was about your age."

"Is he inside the house?"

"No, he died before you were born."

Kate had wanted to tell Eoin about her beloved father, but knew if she had told him about his grandfather and her family, she would have had to explain why she never took him to see his grandmother and uncles.

Opening the garden gate, they walked hand-in-hand to the main entrance. After a moment's hesitation, Kate raised the fox head doorknocker with resolve and firmly hit the brass stud underneath producing a resounding noise throughout the house. They waited.

The maid, a local girl, opened the door surprised at seeing Kate standing there.

"Come in, Miss McCormack," she addressed Kate, wanting to say more but afraid of committing the sin of being too familiar with her mistress' daughter. Only her facial expression attested to her joy of seeing Kate and the child. Kate waited in the drawing room while the maid went to announce the visitors.

On returning from school, Kate would drop all her belongings in the hall and rush to her father's study to experience his embrace and his joy on seeing her.

What would her mother say in discovering she had a young son? With Francis by her side, they would be a family. With a child and no husband, she would be an embarrassment to her mother. If things went well, they would stay a few days, if not, they would take the late train back to Dublin.

Mrs. McCormack entered the drawing room and was impeccably dressed as usual. Kate, with the help of the lane women, who made it possible for her to work nights in a local hospital since shortly before Eoin had turned two years, was glad she had bought them new clothes for this occasion. Eoin, precious child, Kate thought, looked very handsome in his navy blue blazer, gray short pants, knee-high socks, and well polished shoes.

"Kate!" her mother said in surprise. Apparently the maid had not mentioned who the visitors in the drawing room were. Genevieve McCormack walked towards her daughter and embraced her. Kate could not recall ever being embraced in childhood by her mother. "It's good to see you. You are looking well."

"And you too, Mother."

"How did you get here?"

"We took a sidecar from the station."

"Good gracious, one of those dirty old things! Kieran could have picked you up if you had let us know you were coming."

Noticing the maid standing awkwardly at the door waiting for instructions, Genevieve McCormack addressed her.

"Bring some tea, sandwiches and an assortment of those small cakes from the bakery." After the maid left, Kate was about to introduce her son when Kieran knocked and entered the room.

"Kate," he exclaimed on seeing his sister. "What a marvelous surprise, isn't it, Mother? You're looking well. You look better than well, as fantastic as ever."

Kieran's exuberance always made her feel good. As she turned to her mother, she noticed her mother looking at Eoin.

"This is my son, Eoin Francis Egan." Kate announced, suddenly eager to get these make or break details settled.

"You are married!" Kieran said in a voice of congratulations.

"Yes."

"This child is about four or five years old. Yet we have never met your husband, and I gather he is not with you now?" her mother questioned.

"No, Francis is not with us. He works in England."

"How convenient!"

Kate was embarrassed by her mother's observation. She felt like a small child again being reprimanded by her aloof mother. *What am I doing here? Mother believes I'm lying about being married, and with Francis out of my life, that's understandable. I hate this house. After Daddy's death, it was no longer home to me. I should not have returned.*

"Would you like to see my marriage certificate?"

"Kate, what Mom is saying is you never told us you married, or invited us to your wedding. We've never met this man, and now you bring home a child!"

"Not a child. My child." Kate defiantly answered, emboldened by the rejection of her son.

"You named him after Father?" Kieran accused.

"Yes, Daddy would have loved him."

Eoin who had found a child's storybook belonging to one of Kieran's daughters, was sitting in an armchair reading.

"You dishonor his name," her mother told her.

"Momma," the child called out, "can I read this story to you?"

"Not at the moment, Eoin."

"That's Deirdre's book. You cannot read at that level!" Kieran insisted.

"He probably can. Just as Daddy taught me to read, I have taught my son."

"Father thought so highly of you. He would be greatly disappointed by your actions."

"Disappointed, Kieran, maybe, but I believe, unlike you and Momma, he would have accepted his namesake as his grandson."

"You know very little about your father," her mother stated in a flat, tired manner.

The maid arrived with the tea tray, and placed it on the small table. Genevieve immediately poured the tea. Kieran pulled out a chair for Kate, who sat down wishing she were far away from this drawing room with its glazed chintz sofa, armchairs, and drapes. *Just tea and then we'll leave,* she decided.

"Would you like me to read to you?" Eoin asked Kieran.

"No. We're having our tea now."

The boy sat down beside his mother. *Oh, Eoin, love, if there ever was a time to be on your best behavior, it's now. Please don't spill the tea on the linen tablecloth or drops crumbs on the carpet, and above all, I pray, do not chip or break the teacup.*

Her mother and brother ignored Eoin's presence. Before arriving at this house, Kate had requested Eoin remain silent unless spoken to, and he sat wondering who these people were that knew his mother, yet he had never before seen.

"Where do you live?"

"In Dublin, where I've been living all along!"

"I meant," her mother, said with irritation in her voice, "What kind of accommodation do you have? A flat, or a house?"

"A cottage."

"A cottage! One of those little places with thatched roofs? Surely they don't have those in Dublin?"

"No thatched roof." Kate was relieved that her mother did not pursue this conversation any further.

When they had had their tea, Kate mentioned they would take the next train back to Dublin. Her mother seemed sad to see Kate leave yet did not invite her and Eoin to stay, not even overnight. Although Kate did not wish to stay, she was hurt that an invitation to do so was not extended to them. Her mother and brother insisted that Kieran drive them to the train station.

"You need not worry, Momma. I will not walk down Main Street with my scarlet letter walking beside me for all to see, but rather take the old back road past the National School where it is unlikely we'll meet anyone. It is a nice evening for a walk. We did, however, speak with the stationmaster, who brought us into the ticket office to show us the station's first prize ribbon."

"It's blue," Eoin added, since his mother spoke of their joint venture.

Kate and Eoin walked an old dirt road back to the station.

"My shoes are not shiny anymore."

"That's true. This dirt road will make us look less presentable but it doesn't matter now, love. We're going home."

"Do the people in grandfather's house not like us?"

Before Kate could answer, to Kate's relief and Eoin's delight, a dog came running up to them, and jumped up on Eoin causing him to laugh in delight. A man in the distance called to the dog, which turned and ran back, but halfway there, turned again and ran towards Eoin and again jumped up on the boy. The man who had called to the dog, on coming closer to them, suddenly ran towards them and exclaimed, "Kate?"

"Kate McCormack!" he smiled in happy remembrance. Kate smiled at a now slimmed-down Eamon Talbot, looking more handsome than she ever remembered him to have been. "Oh God, Kate, its great to see you."

"This is a lovely surprise!"

"You haven't changed. You're the same delightful person. You've been visiting the family, and I didn't know about it," he said in dismay, looking at her suitcase.

He has changed, marvelously so.

"How long have you been in Gory?"

"Just for the day. We're on our way to the train station."

"Leaving by the back road?"

"I thought we'd go past the old National School on our way back to the station."

"Not many children now in the town. Most of those we knew while growing up are scattered." Then he looked at the boy playing with the dog, he asked, "Your son, I presume?"

"Yes, this is Eoin Egan. Eoin, Mr. Talbot is an old friend of mine."

Eoin stopped playing with the dog long enough to shake Eamon's outstretched hand, and asked, "Is this your dog?"

"Yes, Eoin, his name is Max." The boy once again turned his attention to the dog.

Why am I so deliriously happy to see her? She's married. What might have been can now never be. Yet, I can't just let her walk away.

"May I walk with you both to the train station?" Talbot asked, although he had been going in the opposite direction. They walked the dirt road together. "Your husband didn't come with you?"

"No, he works in England."

After a brief pause, he stated, "You've named the boy after your father?"

"Yes."

"I was always very fond of your father, but then, everyone in Gory was. Now, here you are married and with his grandson."

"Have you married?"

"No, my favorite girl left town."

Not knowing what to say, Kate remained silent.

"Do you think, as I do, that if my parents weren't so anxious for us to marry, and your mother didn't pressure you to do so, we would have had a chance?"

"We'll never know for sure," Kate softly replied, remembering how her mother spoke of Eamon as coming from a 'good family.'

Kate recalled her mother's high estimation of Eamon, the eldest of the Talbots' three children, and his parents' only son. Kate's mother knew Eamon was destined to inherit his parent's pub, an enterprise that would thrive in good times or bad. It would be a good match, Genevieve McCormack had told Kate. His parents were for it, and the quiet, sensitive Eamon was very fond of her and would treat her kindly.

The more her mother pushed Kate into what her mother thought to be a golden opportunity, the more Kate came to dislike not only his family, but his very name which became distasteful to her.

When Kate went to college in Dublin, her mother requested that she write to Eamon. Kate replied, saying her studies consumed all her time. Now looking at this man who walked beside her, Kate saw a very nice young man, no longer a bashful boy, with a background similar to hers. He had grown more interesting in her years away from home, or, she wondered, was he always pleasant and interesting but she did choose not to see it?

Believing Kate to be happily married, Eamon would not pursue what was not his.

The train was already in the station and getting ready to pull out. Eamon lifted the child and hugged him. Putting Eoin down, he turned to Kate and said, "It's been great to see you again even if only for a brief moment," and then he kissed her on the cheek and embraced her.

"Well, Kate, you have it all: a career, marriage, and a delightful child. You deserve the best." He hesitated for a moment, and then added, "If you're ever caught in a storm, Kate, call me; I'll come."

"Thank you, Eamon," She smiled.

If he but knew how much stormy weather I've been through! I cannot burden him with my misadventures. I could have come to him when I found myself pregnant and told him straight out what I had done, and he would have accepted me and my child. Alas, that would have destroyed his life, for small towns never forget the indiscretions of the past, and I would have become Hawthorne's Hester. None of that could have compared to what Eoin would suffer as a bastard child. I could not, would not allow that to happen to my son.

They boarded the train, followed by Max, which forced Eamon to follow. The wayward dog sought the child. Eoin opened the compartment door, and the dog put his paws on Eoin's shoulders, claiming the boy.

"Does he not have a dog?" Eamon asked, reluctantly knowing he must separate the two.

"No, no room for a dog in our very small living quarters."

"I'll pull Max out, and you must close the door," Eamon instructed the boy.

"Here, let me help you, Eoin," his mother stated as each of the three of them struggled to bring to an end that which they would have liked to prolong. Eamon half pulled, half carried the big dog out into the passageway.

"Come back soon," he called to her as he took the reluctant Max from the train. Eoin waved to Max, and Kate waved to Eamon, a solitary figure on the station platform as the train began to pull out of the station.

What could have happened, might have happened could not have happened after my encounter with Harry Brown.

CHAPTER 9

Kate and Eoin had no sooner settled down in their compartment than they heard a knock on the door. Kate opened the compartment door. Her brother Rory was standing there in the doorway with his wife, Gwen. He encircled Kate in an all-embracing hug.

"It's so good to see you again, little sister."

"Hello, Kate," Gwen said, as she squeezed past her husband in order to hug Kate. "We saw a handsome man wave goodbye, and looking down the train from our compartment window, discovered he was waving to you!"

"That was Eamon, an old friend from our school days in Gory."

"Married?"

"No."

"When did you arrive? Have you been to the house?" Rory, in entering the conversation cut off the women's fanciful thinking.

"We arrived today. We've had tea with Momma and Kieran, and now we're on our way back to Dublin."

"Without seeing me?" he asked in playful accusation. "And who is this young man who's sharing your compartment?"

"My son, Eoin."

"Eoin, I'm your Uncle Rory," her brother said scooping the boy up into his arms. "You are as handsome, Eoin, as your mother is beautiful. But why, Kate, are you leaving so soon?"

"We didn't know you were home or would have invited you to our home," Gwen added.

After the reception she had received at her mother's house, Kate wanted to cut short this meeting with Rory before permitting him to condemn her for her past indiscretions. But the manner in which he lifted Eoin into his arms and introduced himself as the child's uncle caused her to hesitate. She thought about the game they used to play as children, calling out "friend or foe" when one of them came into view.

Was Rory's friendship as shallow as Kieran's? As a child, she would eagerly await Kieran's coming home from college. He was her hero. Yet, the one time she came to him for help, he refused her.

"My visit has upset Momma. It was, perhaps, wrong of me to come back. Momma didn't approve of my being seen in public with a child, and I without a husband," Kate told Rory and Gwen, deciding to get it all out in the open and get their reaction.

"Gwen and I would be proud to have you and young Eoin accompany us to the dining carriage. We're on our way to Dublin for the horse show. It's absolutely great seeing you again, Kate."

"Yes," Gwen added, "and since you live in Dublin, we'll be able see a great deal of you during our week there."

"Well, I took three days off to come to Gory, but since I stayed just one day, I have Monday and Tuesday free."

"You must come to the horse show with us every day," Gwen insisted. "We're staying at the Shelburne Hotel on Stephen's Green."

Gwen and Kate followed Rory and Eoin who were heading to the dining car.

Gwen and Rory were not, as her mother would say, "blessed with children." There was disappointment at the time of this discovery, but teaching schedules, faculty functions, students' needs, and the social life the university provided them made for a very active and full life. Not having children of their own left them with the opportunity and resources to do what they both loved—travel to primitive and exotic places. Although they both loved children, they became not so much resigned to, but accustomed to, having no children. They loved each other and were happy in their careers.

Dinner was very pleasant with reminiscence and much laughter. Gwen and Rory's happiness was contagious. Kate enjoyed their company, and Eoin delighted in their attention to him. After they had dessert, Gwen brought forth from her handbag some playing cards. "Do you play cards?" she asked Eoin and when he answered no, she suggested they go back to Uncle Rory's compartment, and she would instruct him in card playing. Their departure left Kate and Rory time alone to talk.

"Tell me, Kate, what has been happening in your life?"

"Well, I'm married to Francis Egan. Eoin was conceived before my marriage to Francis who is therefore not his father. Francis has left me. He's working in England."

"How did you manage? You would have to have left your job before Eoin's birth, and afterwards you had an infant to take care of. How on earth did you manage?"

"Very poorly. Fortunately Francis provided me with a place to stay, but I was without an income for quite a while."

"Why didn't you get in touch with one of us?"

"I did."

"You did! You received money from mother, or money from your inheritance?"

"No. I didn't ask mother. I asked Kieran, who was in touch with Daddy's lawyer, and handled Mother's financial affairs, if I could have advancement on my inheritance from Daddy. If wouldn't be mine, I knew, until I was twenty-five years old, which I will be next month, but I desperately needed some of it at that time."

"And Kieran took care of it?"

"No. He said no advancement was permitted."

"How did you survive without cash?"

"I was greatly helped by the kindness of my neighbors. They also loaned me a crib and a carriage. I gave birth in the cottage to avoid the expense of going to the hospital for delivery, and to avoid the charity wards. I worked in a cinema until two days before Eoin was born"

"The cinema? Doing what?"

"Picking up rubbish between seats, and I was cleaning bathrooms."

"That bastard! He could have gotten you the advancement, yet he put you through all that?"

Rory was angry. Kate wasn't sure if Rory was correct in his assessment of the situation. The money wasn't hers until she became of age to receive it. She had assumed from what Kieran had told her, that the money not accessible.

"I'm back doing nursing part-time. At Christmastime, on the eve before Eoin's first Christmas, I received a Christmas card and a money order from Francis. Every month since, I've gotten a money order from London. He gave his aunt a work telephone number to contract him in an emergency, a number they will not use. Other than that, I have had no contact with him. If I did, I'd tell him I'm working and when I turn twenty-five years next month, I will no longer need his financial support."

"He abandons you, and yet he left his cottage at your disposal? He is a strange one!"

"Is our family not in some ways strange, too?"

"Yes, I must agree with you on that. All families have their peculiarities."

"I should not have come home. Momma always gave me the impression she didn't like me. She never spent time with me; didn't really speak to me. I never seemed to please her.

"You both got off on the wrong foot. Give her another chance."

"No, Rory, she's unhappy enough with me. I'd rather not return and add to her unhappiness." Kate's words rushed forth and then came to a halt. After a brief silence, she asked, "Why doesn't she like me?"

"It was not that she didn't like you. It was what you represented."

"Represented! I am her only daughter!"

"It goes back to before you were born."

"I could hardly have offended anyone before being born!"

The waiter came to the table.

"More wine?" he asked.

"No," Kate replied, "not for me, but I'd like some tea."

"Two teas," Rory said. After the waiter left, Rory revealed some of the family's past history.

"Mom and Dad were not very suited to each other. They had different tastes and interests and incompatible personalities. Mom was caught up in maintaining a beautiful home and in the social life of the town, such as it was. Dad found the party scene where they mingled endlessly with the same people, bore.

Mom discovered he had a friendship with Helena, the librarian. Their relationship apparently consisted of lengthy discussions on politics, history, philosophy, and literature, and as far as anyone knew, all these discussions transpired in the local library. I do not think there was any hanky panky going on; just Dad being able to speak with another person about things that interested him, and which Helena was well qualified to discuss. Whether there was more to it than that I do not know, and neither did Mom, but she sought to end it even though I thought, and believe she also felt, there was nothing happening that should not be happening between Helena and Dad.

"Helena was a very nice person, and did not seem like the home-wrecker type. Kieran and I were about nine and eleven at the time. Mom hadn't wanted any more than two children. She had hoped to have a boy and a girl, but my arrival spoiled that plan.

"In order to 'save' her marriage, Mom got pregnant. Dad's intellectual pursuits were put aside, and he gave into her every wish during her pregnancy. Dad was deliriously happy when you showed up. Mom had always wanted a daughter and was happy until you had passed the infant stage. When you were about a year old, Mom saw all Dad's love centered on you, leaving her on the sidelines. Her sole reason for having another child was to win him back, and now the child, the daughter she always wanted, was the center of Dad's affection.

"Mom could not take it. She fell into a deep depression that lasted over two years. Dad had to hire a nanny to take care of you, because Mom could not do so."

"I don't remember Momma being depressed. She always seemed so strong and capable." Kate said in amazement.

"You were too young to know."

"So that is why she disliked me."

"It wasn't that Mom disliked you. The situation caused enmity between her and you. She didn't want him *not* to love you. She just wanted him to share a portion of that great love he had for you with her."

"Even now I seem to remind her of something she lost."

"Mom would have given you the money you needed. Of course, you wouldn't ask her. Why then didn't you come to me when you needed money?"

"Kieran managed the family finances. After Daddy died, I felt I had nobody to turn to. Kieran always smiled at me, took a moment or two to relate a joke to me as he came and went from the house. Of course, he never stayed long, but the few minutes he spent with me made me happy. So I approached him concerning the advancement."

"He smiled at you! Shared a joke with you! That was all you required? Then I failed you. I tried to step into Dad's shoes where you were concerned."

"I don't know whose shoes you stepped into, Rory, but they certainly weren't Daddy's shoes," Kate laughed. "Daddy trusted me. He believed in me. Believed I'd do what was right."

"Stepping in for Dad was a tough job that I had assigned myself, and with the arrogance of a twenty-year old."

"You did what you thought best. Taking Daddy's place in my life would have been beyond anyone's ability."

"I was new at the job and a bit heavy-handed, I must admit."

"A bit heavy-handed," Kate laughed. "You had absolutely no faith in me. You questioned my every movement, didn't like my friends, and demanded an account of where I had been, whom I was with, and what took place. You missed your calling, Rory. You had the makings of a diligent detective."

"Was I that bad? It was all done to protect you," he explained.

"From what?"

"Well, you were much too friendly with the Gillespie boys, and they were trouble."

"Yes, they were pranksters, but they were never into any serious trouble."

"Oh, you don't think so? Tying two door knobs together and knocking on both doors simultaneously so that when the people tried to open their front doors, they each pulled against the other and neither door would open?"

"That was a Hallows Eve prank."

"What about the summer they tied two cats' tails together, then threw the cats over a clothesline where the cats scratched each other almost to death?"

"The Gillespie's didn't do that."

"Is that what they said?"

"No, I was with them when that happened, and we were nowhere near Mrs. Davitt's clothesline. By the time we heard about it, Tom Payne had cut the twine and released the cats. The Gillespies were blamed for many things they were not involved in. Some 'nice boys' from good families, whose mothers thought butter wouldn't melt in their mouths, did the really nasty things."

"Well, maybe I misjudged them, but I didn't want your reputation sullied by your association with them."

Kate laughed and laughed.

"What's so funny?"

"The voice is yours but those words are Momma's—'my reputation, 'sullied through association.'"

"All right, I'm a pompous ass."

"No, Rory, you were just overcautious to the point of making me feel badly about myself. The only person I had to talk to other than Sheila, who was two years older than me and hung out with her age group, was Ronan Gillespie. He was such a nice person and friend, and he wasn't judgmental. Sometimes I think Dad sent him into my life just when I needed a friend."

"There were three of you that were always together: Ronan, his brother and yourself."

"Yes, his little brother hung around with us because his mother worked cleaning people's houses, and he didn't want to be alone at home. He didn't even remember his father, but Ronan did. And so we talked about our fathers. Nobody in the family spoke of Daddy to me. Sometimes, I thought, nobody cared that he was gone from our lives. And yes, I was perfectly safe in the Gillespie brothers' company."

"You were only a child. A kind word and a smile was what you needed, not my heavy-handedness."

"And I, Rory, I unfortunately misjudged you," Kate said apologetically.

"Our Comedy of Errors," Rory laughed.

"It's over and done with now, Rory. The fourth of September I'll be twenty-five years old. So, in one-month's time, I will receive my inheritance. So, 'All's Well that Ends Well.'"

"Congratulations! What are your plans for this sum of money?"

"There's talk that the government is going to demolish the cottages in the lane. I don't know if there is any truth to this rumor. Eventually I plan to buy a house. If this rumor becomes a fact, I'll be doing it earlier than expected. Of course, if this all comes about, the government will have to find homes for all the families living in the lane, and that will take time."

"Why do they want to demolish those cottages?"

"For health reasons. They contend that too many people are living in such small dwellings. Such was so years ago when these cottages housed large families. Now, except for two families, they house couples whose children have married and left home, and a few people living alone."

"Where—"

"Momma, Momma," called Eoin as he raced into the dining compartment, "Aunt Gwen and I saw the engineer shovel the coal into the fire to make the train go. He was all sooty, even his face. He let me throw in some coal."

"Yes, and we've washed our hands and faces since we participated in that activity," Gwen laughed.

"Let's stay together during our five days in Dublin," Rory proposed. Since you have a small cottage, please accept Gwen's and my invitation to you and Eoin to join us at our hotel. I'll take care of all the arrangements."

"Yes, do say yes," Gwen urged.

"That's very kind of you both, but I only have two more days before I must return to work."

"Then we'll make the most of your two days with us, and whatever time you have available after work." Turning to Eoin, Rory asked, "Do you like horses?"

"Yes, sir."

"That's yes, Uncle Rory, for you are my one and only nephew. I do believe, Eoin, you'll enjoy the Dublin Horse Show. Maybe someday you'll ride a horse as competently as your Mommy."

"Eoin rides a horse on his granduncle's farm, as do I whenever the opportunity of a visit presents itself. When he starts school, I'll work full time, Eoin will spend summers on the farm, and I will be there on my days off."

"Who is this granduncle?" Rory wished to know.

"They are Francis' uncle Ned and his aunt Mary who live on a farm. They are a wonderful couple and were the first family members I introduced to Eoin when he was just a few months. Eoin is the joy of their lives."

"Acceptance!"

"Immediate and complete," said Kate.

"Eoin, let's you and I find the train map and see where we are on the map." Gwen suggested. Eoin was happy to do so, and they left.

"It must have been obvious to Ned and Mary that whatever family I had, I was an outcast to them. Other than that I do not know what they thought of the situation. Our wedding reception took place in their home. Mary, with the aid of her neighbors and friends, prepared the wedding feast. Ned drove the four of us to the church in his side-car. It was a beautiful event." A moment of silence followed.

"My not revealing my condition destroyed what Francis and I had."

"That's partly true, but the other part was *his* reaction to the news you imparted to him."

"He believed I married him solely to give the child a father, and that was true. However, I fell in love with Francis almost immediately. He disregarded that part."

Before Rory would speak, Eoin and Gwen return with the names of all the train stops before reaching Dublin.

"Umm, I have a feeling, Eoin, that you and your Mommy have been to the horse show before."

"Yes," the boy answered gleefully. "Momma took me every year even when I was a baby."

"She has? Have you ever stayed in a hotel before?"

"I don't think so. Where is that?"

"A hotel is a place to sleep and eat when you're away from home."

"I don't think we've ever been there, have we, Momma?"

"No. We've stayed at the farm, but that's with family, not a hotel."

"It will be a new experience for you, Eoin," laughed Rory.

During a late dinner, after two unforgettable days with Rory and Gwen, Rory insisted on taking Kate and Eoin home by taxi, although Kate told him they could get a bus home. With the four of them in a taxi, they arrived at the bottom of the lane after dark.

The taxi stopped.

"Well, why isn't he going up the lane?"

"Too narrow. No cars allowed," Kate told Rory.

Gwen and Rory wished to escort them up the lane, while the taxi driver waited as instructed. It was a beautiful clear August evening. The lane was as quiet as an empty church. A cool breeze, as always, but much more appreciated in summer than winter, drifted in from the sea. Gwen and Rory studied the surroundings as they passed the water pump and turned towards the cottages, the only sound being their footsteps.

Some candles had been lit and were shedding a soft mellow glow into the lane. The front of the cottages having just one small window made nightfall seem earlier inside the cottages than outside. On arriving at her cottage, Kate opened the door, stepped inside, and lit a candle before inviting her family in.

"How utterly quaint," Gwen said in delight, as she entered.

"Where's the light switch?" Rory asked.

"No electricity."

"This is straight out of a child's nursery stories. Absolutely enchanting," Gwen added.

"Would you like some tea?"

"No, we had better go now that we have delivered you safely home. The taxi driver awaits," Rory reminded them.

"Goodnight, Kate. The last two days have been wonderful. We'll pick you up after work tomorrow morning at the hospital and have dinner together each night before our return home."

Then after a brief pause, Gwen asked, "Could Eoin come stay with us overnight?"

"Would you like to stay in a hotel tonight with Uncle Rory and Aunt Gwen?" Kate asked her son.

The boy considered his mother's questions.

"Will you be there?"

"No, I must work tonight, but I'd see you after work tomorrow."

The boy agreed to go with his uncle and aunt. It might prove to be a nice change from being with his mother's friend Monica who took care of him, as did other women in the lane, while his mother worked. Eoin delighted in having an adult male in the group, especially one who paid him much attention, and Gwen was lavish in her praise of Eoin.

After much hugging, they left. Kate, now alone in the cottage, missed her son but was happy that Eoin was secure enough to be able to spend time without her with people he had just recently met. After they had left, Kate, grabbing soap and a towel, walked up the lane, showered and put on her uniform and then sat on the rocking chair, for she dare not asleep as she had the midnight to seven o'clock shift at the hospital. What great parents Gwen and Rory would make, Kate thought as she recalled the day's events.

Gwen, Rory and Eoin were waiting for Kate as she left the hospital after washing and changing out of her uniform and into a dress. Eoin's face had a smile of delight when he saw his mother. Previous to this separation, Eoin remained in the lane while Kate worked, and he knew his mother would always return to the lane. This time there was uncertainty, for he would not be in the lane but, rather, staying in a strange place.

"I was afraid you might forget I was in the hotel place, not the lane," he said all in one breath as he reached up and threw his arms around his mother. As they stood clinging to each other, Rory broke the connection.

"Let's go back to the hotel where you can have some breakfast, Kate, and can sleep while we take this young man sightseeing. We'll pick you up at about one o'clock for lunch, then head for the horse show. Does this meet with everyone's wishes?"

"Sounds perfect to me," Kate answered.

"And me," Gwen replied.

On a gloriously sunny August day without a cloud in the sky, Gwen and Rory, Kate and Eoin entered the horse show grounds amid elegantly dressed women in summer gowns wearing wide brim picture hats, accompanied by their equally elegantly dressed escorts. Gwen and Kate watched this parade of fashion with fascination while Rory studied the racing form, though he was not immune to the glamour in their midst.

At the sound of a horn by a lone rider on horseback who entered the ring conversation and laughter was cut short, and all eyes turned as horses and riders commenced to fill the ring. Riders from France, Germany, Spain, the Netherlands, Belgium, Italy, Ireland, and England, splendidly dressed in riding outfits, and Americans in military uniforms, began their walk around the ring as the national anthem of each country was played. Each saluted the Irish president as they passed the grandstand.

Each team, hoping to win the Aga Khan cup for their country, jumped over hurdles, ditches, water, barricades, all of which followed a zigzag route between obstacles placed nicely apart and others very close together and some that had to be jumped at an angle or after a sharp turn. A hush lay over the crowd as each jump was made, followed by a burst of applause on the completion of a perfect jump. As the jumps were made higher, the tension rose among the crowd, for the riders had not only to steady their horses for the more difficult jumps, but they were racing against time. A combination of perfect jumps and the shortest time completing the round decided the winner.

People attending this sporting event usually had a favorite rider they cheered on. A particular rider who had won or had an almost perfect performance in previous years would be guaranteed much support from the crowd. A British rider held the honor for a few years, and people spoke of him as though they knew him well, calling him by his first name.

After the afternoon's spectacular performance, Rory suggested they go to the stables so that Eoin could see some of the horses up close. They walked through throngs of people to the stables, where they found the horses being rubbed down and fed. Many stalls were empty as the horses had not yet returned to their stalls. They chatted as they looked into the stalls along the way.

Rory suddenly realized that Eoin was not among them. They looked in both directions and not seeing him, Rory backtracked to all the empty stables. As he did so, Kate told Gwen she would walk in the direction they had not yet covered, and they could meet back at the stall where they first discovered Eoin had disappeared.

As she walked, Kate called out her son's name. Coming to a

wooden barrier that bore the sign, "Private—no admittance," Kate stopped. Deciding that such a sign would not prevent a four-year-old child with a great curiosity from entering, she climbed over the fence that Eoin could easily have climbed under and continued her search.

Eoin, who did not consider himself lost, came upon a beautiful chestnut color horse being rubbed down in its stall. He had been standing there for several minutes admiring the horse before the groom became aware of his presence.

"How did you get here? You're not allowed in this area," the groom stated.

Undaunted by these words, Eoin stood in awe of this magnificent creature. Reaching out his hand, he rubbed it along the horse's shank.

"Can I climb up on him?"

"That's not allowed," the groom, answered as another man entered the stall.

"Who do we have here, Mike?"

"I don't know where he came from, Mr. Fitzgerald, but this young fellow wants to mount 'Our Own.'"

"What's your name, son?"

"Eoin Egan, sir. Is this your horse? May I sit on him?"

"Egan!"

"I told him it was out of the question. He's a stubborn one, he is."

"Well now, Mike, I'd like to make an exception in this case," and turning to the child asked, "So you'd like to sit on him."

"Yes, sir." Reaching down, Fitzgerald picked the boy up and placed him on the horse. Eoin smiled in delight.

"Do you ride?"

"Yes, sir," Eoin answered. "I ride a pony on my granduncle's farm." Then seeing his mother turn into the stall area, he called out to her. "Look Momma!"

"Mrs. Egan, I presume," Fitzgerald said as he raised his cap. "I'm Brian Fitzgerald."

Kate, who had never met Fitzgerald in person, was momentarily taken back.

"Your son has taken a fancy to our horse."

Yes, she recognized him from newspaper photographs, and memories of Harry's dispute all came flooding back to her.

"We must go now, Eoin," Kate said as she reached up for her son who reluctantly slid off the horse into her arms. "Thank you, Mr. Fitzgerald, for your kindness to my son."

"But, Momma, I want to sit on him."

"He's a fine lad, Mrs. Egan. Now, Eoin lad, listen to your Momma."

As Kate took her son by the hand, Fitzgerald, said, "It's been very nice meeting you, Mrs. Egan."

"And in my meeting you, Mr. Fitzgerald."

As Kate and Eoin walked back to where she had left Gwen, Kate told Eoin he must never wander off from her. To which he replied, "But Momma, I remembered what you said. If I get lost I should ask a policeman to help me find you, and I should tell him my name and where I live."

"Yes, Eoin, that is correct. However, you must not walk away from me without telling me where you are going."

This was all very confusing to Eoin who had not left the stable area, and felt he had only to walk back and join his mother, aunt and uncle after he had checked out the remaining stalls.

"You must promise me this won't happen again."

"I promise."

A young woman walked towards them. Kate immediately recognized Kit Fitzgerald from the society pages of the newspaper. *She is a much prettier woman in person,* Kate thought as they came face-to-face. She is probably wondering what Eoin and I are doing coming out of the area that warns "No Admittance." Kit smiled and wished them "a good afternoon" as she passed by. Kate answered in kind.

CHAPTER 10

The week they had together had come to an end all too soon. When Eoin discovered his newfound family would be leaving Dublin, he asked why they could not continue to live at the hotel, so that they might all see each other. Rory explained that he and Gwen had to go home and prepare for the new school year that would start in September. Eoin, who was impatiently waiting for the day he could enter school, understood.

It had been a memorable week. While Eoin had come to know his uncle, Kate and Gwen had enjoyed shopping and lunching together. Kate was saddened to say goodbye, but was extremely happy that she had come to know and understand Rory better, and happy also for the lovely relationship that had developed between her and Gwen.

A fortnight had passed since Rory and Gwen had spent a week in Dublin. Arriving alone, Rory knocked on the brass doorknocker of his mother's house. The maid on opening the door smiled and said, "Good afternoon, Mr. McCormack."

"Good afternoon to you, Sarah. Is my mother home?"

"Yes, sir. I'll go fetch her for you," and she hurried to find his mother.

A smile spread over Rory's face as he wondered what his mother would think of Sarah's words. "To fetch," as a dog might fetch a stick or the morning newspaper; but fetch his regal mother! But then, he figured, all Sarah needed do was use the proper wording in his mother's presence, a task she must have acquired for Sarah had remained for the longest time of any maid in his mother's employment. All Sarah's brothers and sisters had married, leaving her, the youngest and unmarried in the family homestead, to keep her widowed father company and tend to his needs.

"Rory," Kieran said as he stepped into the room where Rory stood. "To what or to whom do we owe this visit?"

"Kieran, have you taken up permanent residence here? If so, why are your wife and children not here with you?"

"I've come to visit Mom. That's something you rarely do."

Genevieve McCormack on entering the room addressed them.

"Aren't you boys ever going to grow up to the point of being able to converse in a civilized manner?"

"You're looking well, Mother." Looking around him he added, "Have you ever thought of selling this great, big, drafty old house, and getting something smaller?"

"This is my home." Genevieve answered with the coldness and sharpness of an icicle.

"It was a great house for us to grow up in," Rory said, "but now that you live alone, I thought, it might be too much for you to take care of. Besides, half of the rooms are closed off."

"They are dusted and vacuumed weekly."

"But not used?"

"My brother, who seldom comes to visit, is now telling us the house should be sold!"

"Only a suggestion. Nothing more."

"You didn't come here, Rory, to make suggestions about the house," his mother stated.

"True, Mom. Gwen and I spent the week of the August holiday in Dublin with Kate and her young son."

Genevieve McCormack received this news in silence, and then as though he had said Kate was gravely ill, asked, "How is Kate?"

"She is doing well now. She's now working part-time at a hospital in Dublin. She's been through a very difficult time. She's had to wash toilets in a cinema up to two days before the birth of her child in order to survive."

"Good Lord, Rory, why didn't she come to one of us for help?"

"She did. She asked Kieran for advancement on her inheritance, but he told her that was out of the question until she was twenty-five years old."

"That's nonsense," she replied now turning to Kieran. "Why didn't you tell me she came to you for money?"

"Dad specified age twenty-five so her inheritance wouldn't be squandered away. She didn't say why she needed the money. How was I to know she was in such desperate straights?"

"How very judgmental of you! You forced our sister to give birth in a small unheated two-room cottage without indoor plumbing instead of in a hospital."

"She could have died!" their mother uttered in horror.

"Perhaps you should sit down, Mom," Rory said lifting a chair and bringing it towards her. She sat down and leaned back into the chair with her arms resting on the armrests.

"Would you like water, Mom, or a cup of tea?" Rory asked. She waved her hand, rejecting this suggestion. After a few moments, she spoke.

"How could you have treated my daughter, your only sister, so horribly?"

"When Kate came to visit, you didn't exactly welcome her," Kieran declared in his own defense. "You were more concerned about what the neighbors might think."

"Yes, and for that I am ashamed. From the moment she left this house that day, I regretted my actions." Looking at Rory she asked, "Was she alone giving birth?"

"No. Her neighbors were there to help her."

"How can they help her? They must be rather poor to live in that place. After her father died, Kate seemed drawn to the disadvantaged in life, like the Gillespie boys. It embarrassed me that she neglected her respectable friends to do so."

"In our grief, we pretty much ignored Kate. Ronan Gillespie had lost his father, and so she could speak to him about her own loss."

"She lived among that kind of people in Dublin?"

"Mom, she was poorer than they were, and pregnant."

"Kieran, why did you not inform me? I would have given her the money she needed," Genevieve said, not so much as an accusation as in disappointment and sadness. She rose from the chair saying, "I'll have Sarah bring us in some tea." After she left the room, Kieran spoke.

"What I did was follow the terms of Dad's will."

"What you did was despicable."

"How come she didn't go to you, brother?"

"She got her 'friends and foes' mixed up. Of course, she never knew how angry you were when Dad's will was read and you found he left his money: a third to Mom, a third to Kate and a third to be divided equally between you and me. You thought the remaining two thirds should have been divided equally between the three of us. So you made Kate pay for Dad's generosity to her."

"Is that true?" Genevieve asked from the doorway.

"Of course not, Mother. It's just Rory's way of making things difficult for me. Sure, I was upset at the time that Dad did not divide his money evenly among the three of us, but that certainly had nothing, *nothing whatsoever*, to do with my upholding Dad's wish that Kate's inheritance remain intact until she was twenty-five years old. And I can honestly state, I did not know how much she needed the money at that time."

"Nevertheless, I'm appalled that you kept Kate's request for money from me."

"But, Mom . . ."

Kieran's words were cut off by the maid's knock on the door. As requested she brought in the tea tray. An awkward silence transpired while the maid put down the tray, asking if anything else was required, and then left the room.

Does this girl think we just sit here silently looking at each other, Rory wondered. *What did she think when Kate and Eoin came to visit? She, no doubt, couldn't wait to leave that day and spread all the news and her version of what was happening at the McCormack house. Someone has to break the silence; Mom's statement that we should help ourselves doesn't count.*

"Well, Kieran, how are your girls?"

"You'd know how they were doing if you came to visit Mom more often. We're here for dinner every Sunday."

"Every Sunday! That doesn't give you much of an opportunity to reciprocate?"

"Mom spends Christmas Eve and Christmas day with my family. You don't even visit your nieces at Christmas. Last Christmas you and Gwen spent a week in Austria skiing and spent the previous Christmas in Paris."

"Well, this year we plan to be in Ireland for Christmas, and Gwen and I invite all the family to join us."

"I told you, Mom always comes to our home for Christmas."

Putting his teacup down Rory praised his mother, "Good tea, Mom. Under your guidance, Sarah has learned to make an excellent cup of tea. I must leave now."

He rose and kissed his Mother on the cheek, and gave his brother a friendly whack on the back which caused him to double over. "Perhaps this Christmas the whole family can get together. Would that not be a grand celebration?" Rory said, as he walked towards the door and, closing it behind him, left the house.

"Do you think Uncle Rory and Aunt Gwen have 'Trick or Treat' at their house?"

"I'm sure they do. With a college full of students, I'd say it is a big celebration."

"I don't want to be a ghost with a pillow case over my head again, Mom."

"What would you like to dress as this year?"

"A pirate."

"So it shall be," his mother laughed.

"That's great," Eoin enthused while jumping up and down. "What will I wear?"

"Well, there's that chair leg out in the woodpile we could fix into a peg leg for you. I have a scarf we can tie around your head, and I can tape the toasting fork over your hand as a crook. I've put a cork into the fire to blacken, and I'll remove it just before supper so it will be cool enough to draw a big moustache on your face and some big bushy eyebrows. I'll lend you a big earring, but you must not lose it or my head scarf."

"Wait 'til David and Michael see my costume. Will they be surprised!"

"What will they be dressed as?"

"I don't know. Their mother said she would look for something. Tommy isn't dressing up this year. He said he's too old to do that sort of thing any more."

"Eoin, Grandfather O'Toole stopped by today. He asked that you and your friends don't forget to go to his cottage tonight."

"They're scared to, Mom."

"Well, you're not scared of him, are you?"

"No."

"He bought a bag of apples and nuts especially to hand out to-night. You must go and make a call to his cottage, and bring your friends with you."

"Mom is the supper ready yet? I want to get dressed up."

"You have time," Kate laughed at her son's eagerness for the fun to begin.

After supper, Kate tied Eoin's leg back from the knee with a leather belt that had once belonged to Francis. *I hope he will not fall and hurt himself. If he were a girl, I could have dressed him as a gypsy girl in a flowing skirt and shawl or some other safe costume instead of having him hobble around on a chair leg.*

When I was growing up, Mom always had a Snow White or some such non-inspired costume made for me, which I always felt foolish wearing. She was aghast the All Hallows Eve I said I wanted to be Cinderella. It was out of the question, of course, as Mom would have purchased the material for my costume and given it to the seamstress weeks ahead of time.

"Hold still, Eoin, until I get the curl of this moustache on your cheeks."

Hearing a knock, Eoin, called out, "Come in." Michael and David entered wearing some hand-me-down clothes on loan from their uncle who shared the cottage with them.

"You boys are early."

"My mother said we were to get out before we drove her crazy," David answered for both of them.

"I see. So you're both tramps this year?"

"Yes. Mom said we ruined her mother's clothes that we wore last year. It wasn't as though Grandma was going to wear them again. She's been dead since before we were born. But Mom said one never knows when someone might need a couple of black dresses," David explained, again speaking for his brother who could have passed for Walt Disney's dwarf Bashful, without need for a costume. "Why does Eoin call Old Man O'Toole Grandpa?"

"You've just spoken the reason." In answer to the quizzical look on the boys' faces, Kate explained. "Respect for your elders. I don't want Eoin to call this gentleman, Old Man O'Toole, and Grandpa seems appropriate."

"Can we call him Grandpa, too?"

"I can't think of any reason why not. I just mentioned to Eoin before you arrived that Mr. O'Toole would enjoy a visit from you all."

"But we never go to his cottage!"

"Well, tonight is a good time to start doing so."

"Might he chase us away?"

"I wouldn't think so. I saw him around noontime today, and he had a bag of lovely shiny apples and some nuts," Kate answered, although she had not actually seen the apples but had faith in O'Toole's word.

"Come on let's go, Eoin," David said, anticipating an adventure.

"Don't go past the water tap," Kate told Eoin.

"Can we not go the houses on the street at the end of the lane?" David asked.

"Well," she paused to count the houses. "If you stay together and are careful crossing the road, you can go to the six houses on this side and the five houses on the other side, making just one trip across, and one trip back."

The boys were delighted at the thought of all the loot they were about to receive, and left the cottage—a merry band on Trick and Treat night.

This was the night Eoin O'Toole changed his image for the people of the lane. True, he would not socialize with the people after that night was spent, but the memory lingered on, and they smiled at him when they saw him pass by. To the children he became "Grandpa" from that evening onwards. If one looked carefully, when "Grandpa" was spoken, one could catch a smile on Eoin O'Toole's face.

In late autumn, the lone figure of an elegantly-dressed mature woman walked up the lane. She hesitated a few steps after the water tap for she saw no names or numbers on the doors, not that she knew what number she was looking for, but the taxi driver had assured her this was the place as he dropped her off at the bottom of the lane. The anonymity of the place seemed to silently say "intruders keep out."

She was an intruder! Her very shoes objected to walking on cobblestones. Trying to avoid breaking the heels of her shoes, Genevieve walked with an unnatural stride, assuming there were no witnesses to her ungainly steps.

What am I doing in this backward place? After much wavering back and forth, I made the decision. All I need to do now is find Kate's cottage, take her and the child to lunch, discuss matters, and leave from the city without returning to this dreadful place.

A woman, wearing a wrap-around apron, with a basin of sudsy water held by both hands and balanced on her hip, looked surprised to see her. While Genevieve McCormack decided whether to ask this woman for information or not, the woman passed by and emptied the water down the drain, and washed the basin. Now holding the basin with one hand, the woman was about to disappear behind one of these unmarked doors when Genevieve spoke.

"Excuse me. I'm not sure I have the right place. I'm looking for Kate McCormack."

"Kate, who?"

"Sorry. She's now Kate Egan, and she has a small son."

"Oh, Kate. She's in number eight, but she's at work. I'm Monica, a friend of Kate's. She'll be home in about an hour."

"I'm her mother."

"It's nice to meet you," Monica said, as though they might quickly become friends, and extended her hand to the older woman, clasping Mrs. McCormack's white-gloved hand in her own. "Here, let me show you, it's the fourth house down," the woman said leading the way. She unlatched the door and opened it to allow Genevieve to enter. "Young Eoin is in Peg's house. I'll go get him so you can wait with your grandson."

"No," Genevieve said, too abruptly to the point of embarrassing herself. *What grandmother wouldn't want to see her grandson while waiting for her daughter? Children are very observant. I had not spoken to the child when Kate and he came to visit me. How much of our conversation did he hear or understand?. He would have tuned into the sound of our voices, which weren't friendly. What if this woman brought him and he ran out of the cottage to be away from me?*

The woman put the washbasin on the floor.

"Would you like a cup tea?"

"Yes. Thank you." But Genevieve made no attempt to make it. She sat down. Whereupon, Monica poured water from the large enamel water jug into the teakettle and turned on the gas jet underneath it. Then opening the cupboard she took out a cup, saucer, plate, and spoon and placed them on the table. After putting the sugar on the table, she discovered the milk jug was empty.

"She's out of milk, which is not a problem. I'll go down to my cottage and get you some."

"No, please, I can drink it black."

"It wouldn't be any trouble."

But the older woman politely raised her gloved hand in protest.

Monica would have appreciated the small break, for she was perplexed as to what to do for this woman who seemed so uncomfortable and out of place in Kate's cottage. After the water came to a boil, Monica scalded the teapot and then threw the water into a basin. She opened the tea canister and put in two rounded teaspoons to make two cups and an extra teaspoon for the pot and poured in the scolding hot water. Putting the pot on a hot part of the stove away from the flame, she covered it with a tea-cozy and let it brew. She felt the woman's eyes on her every move. *It's not natural,* she thought, *for a grandmother not to want to see her grandchild! People with money have strange ways. Why does this woman, whose clothes look like they were bought on Grafton Street, have a daughter who works so hard to make ends meet?* Monica cut some homemade brown bread and put it on a plate for Genevieve. Taking the butter off the shelf, she placed it on the table.

"Well, enjoy your tea. I'll be getting myself home now," and picking up her basin, she left the house.

As soon as Monica left, Genevieve got up from the chair and looked around for a calendar in the hope that her grandson's birthday would be marked on it. She found none.

After she had finished the first cup of tea, Genevieve wondered where the bathroom might be. She opened the door to the left, but saw it was a bedroom. Was this the room Kate gave birth in? After several moments she closed the door on all that had taken place in that room. Not finding a toilet inside the cottage, she opened the back door which led into a small yard, but none was there either. That's it—nothing more. *Why,* she thinks, *when we gave Kate everything, did she end up a pauper?*

Genevieve looked at a wedding picture of a time long past that stood on a shelf. *No wedding picture of Kate or this man she is supposed to be married to. Who is the boy on the pony? There he is again with the bridal couple, now in work clothes standing on each side of him. And here is the boy again with the same couple and another couple.*

No photographs of Kate or her son. He's a handsome boy. I wish I had acted better towards him on our first meeting. I was so angry with Kate. My only daughter married, and she hadn't invited me, her own mother, to her wedding. She gave birth to a child who was already walking and talking before she informed me of his existence. From what Rory told me, it's all quite complicated. Her son is not the child of her husband. It seemed she was pregnant when she got married. Why did her husband leave her before the child was born? Could it be that he did not know she was pregnant when they married?

I was so happy when Kate was born. I had what I always wanted—a daughter. I envisioned us in the years ahead becoming best friends.

Helping herself to a second cup of tea, she cut and buttered some more bread. Genevieve noted this bread was not her own recipe, *but it was good; very good,* she thought. *It's probably a recipe from that awful woman who used to cook for us. She loved Kate and Kate her. She didn't mind Kate's endless questions or when she messed up in the kitchen. Rather she encouraged it. She was a foul-mouthed woman who didn't know her place and was disrespectful, but she had the patience of a saint with children. And in her kitchen, Kate was her enthusiastic student.*

Kate's father wasn't a fussy eater. One could put anything on a plate before him, and he'd eat it. He usually left all domestic affairs to me, but he forbade me to fire that cook. That, of course, caused me to dislike her even more.

Eoin took Kate from me. He told her she could become whatever she wanted, when the only possibilities open to her were the medical field: nurse, or doctor, or teaching. I made special trips to Dublin to buy her clothes. It broke my heart when I bought her that expensive sapphire blue mohair sweater which looked beautiful on her, only to discover she gave it to the ragman who came around collecting old clothes. Her father did not back me up on that. He merely said, "She obviously didn't like it as much as you did."

I can't wait another moment! Two cups of tea and no bathroom! Walking out the back door, she looked around her. There she saw a drain, a rain barrel, a wood shed and a wall about eight feet high surrounding the yard. *Kate has reduced me to this intolerable situation. What facilities does she use? The wall is high. There is nothing except the squawking seagulls overhead.* Yet Genevieve McCormack was reluctant to expose any part of her body.

The other end of the lane! Yes, that must be where the showers and toilets are situated. Alas, it is too late for a slow torturous trip up the lane in shoes that wobbled and threatened to sprain the ankles. Kate, you have brought me down to a level of discomfort and embarrassment, which previous to this I have never had to endure.

Genevieve remembered walking in the countryside as a child with her parents, and when the need presented itself, there was always the privacy of hedges. Now she must use the drain. Afterwards she would pour some water from the jug into the wash hand bowl, wash her hands, and throw the water down the drain.

Genevieve remembered her father being firm with her when she was a child. Eoin, however, never found fault with Kate. *I was the one that had to discipline her. Then after he died, Kate began associating with those unsavory Gillespie boys, who Rory tells me were nice children.*

I may have been wrong about not consulting Kate on the clothes she wore, but she was too young to know what clothing best suited her. Kate's life would have been much, much better if she had married Eamon Talbot. He loved her. He is a good and caring man. She would have remained in Gory where she belonged. I could have planned her wedding. I would have been with her at the birth of their child, and given her all the help she needed. If Eoin had not spoiled her and taken her away from me, we could have been best friends.

Kate didn't come to me when she found herself pregnant. Can't say I blame her. I thought only very loose and stupid girls got pregnant without marriage. My beautiful daughter is neither stupid nor immoral. How could a man have treated Kate like that man did? How differently we see things when they land on our own doorsteps. Her father would have handled this situation much better. He would have welcomed her home with a loving hug. I couldn't manage that. I don't recall either of my parents ever hugging me. This lack of mine must have hurt Eoin who effortlessly reach out to the children and me. His grandfather would have loved little Eoin. But then Eoin would have doted on any child of Kate's regardless of how it came it entered the world.

Will little Eoin like the special gift I've brought for him? But then, I've brought it more to establish a relationship with my daughter than as a gift for the child.

Suddenly the door was thrust open. Eoin burst in and came to an abrupt halt when he saw his grandmother. Then he rushed out leaving the door open. She could hear the hurried words of warning coming from the child, "Momma, the lady that doesn't like us is in our cottage."

Kate uttered something that Genevieve could not hear. *Momma here? What could possibly have happened to bring her here?*

Kate hurried forward expecting some sort of disaster. Entering the cottage, Kate put down the bottle of milk she had been carrying, and turning to her mother, softly asked. "Is everything all right, Momma?"

"Yes, but obviously not between the boy and myself."

"He only met you once, and it was not a good occasion," Kate suddenly feeling tired, answered flatly. She suppressed the urge to raise her voice and state, *I thought something horrible had happened and all you can offer in response to the fright you gave me is that your relationship with my son is not a particularly good one.*

"What a bad impression I left. Perhaps if he'll let me, I can improve on that first impression."

Kate looked at her son and smiled. "Let's begin over again."

"Momma, this is my son, Eoin."

"It is nice to meet you again, and I hope we can be friends," his grandmother said as she shook hands with the boy.

"Eoin, this is your grandmother."

"Hello, Grandmother."

"Well, now that's a good beginning," Kate smiled.

"I brought you a birthday present," Genevieve said, taking it out of her shopping bag. The shape of the wrapped gift revealed its contents. Yet the boy patiently unwrapped the hurling stick. In the bottom of the bag was the ball.

"Well, do you already have a hurling stick and ball?" Genevieve asked the boy.

Not wanting to displease this strange woman, Eoin looked at his mother, who rescued him.

"Now that you have two sticks, you can keep one here and the other at the farm instead of bringing the hurling stick back and forth on the bus," Kate told her son with enthusiasm, and he smiled at her.

"Should I leave the one Grandpa Eoin gave me at the farm with Grandpa Ned and Grandma Mary, or should I leave this new one there?" Eoin asked, unaware of the confusion he was creating.

"That is your choice, Eoin." Kate smiled.

Genevieve was perplexed. *Grandpa Eoin! There's some mix-up.*

"Kate, what is the child talking about? The grandparents at the farm are your husband's relatives, I presume, but his grandpa Eoin is dead!"

"No, he's not," the boy answered angrily. "No, he's not," Eoin repeated, and put the hurling stick and ball back in the bag. With his foot he pushed it towards Genevieve.

Kate intervened.

"An old man who lives a few cottages up from ours known as Old Man O'Toole, or Old O, is Mr. Eoin O'Toole. He is a very good and kind person and has been a tremendous help to me. He is also a close relative of Francis. Because of this, and also because I did not want Eoin referring to him as Old O, Eoin calls him Grandpa Eoin, which is an apt name for this man we've both come to love."

Genevieve sat quietly in the chair thinking. *My daughter and grandson have a life apart from me, a life that I have had no part of.* Her wish was to establish closer ties to her daughter, but she was feeling more cut off from her than ever. Then she remembered the other gift. Opening her handbag, she took out a small box and handed it to Kate.

"I want my grandson to have this, and I wish you to give it to him when he is old enough to receive it."

Kate opened the unwrapped elegant box and gasped when she saw what it contained.

"Daddy's pocket watch!"

"When the boys were young, and we were living in Dublin, he had a very busy practice and did not have much time for them.

We moved a few years before you were born, and his practice took on an easier pace. He taught you how to tell time with this pocket watch."

"Yes, he would open it and ask that I tell him the time. Oh, Momma, I haven't seen this watch in so long." Tears flooded her eyes. "You want my son to one day own this watch?"

Genevieve nodded in response.

Momma had come here to a place she must have had difficulty finding to make amends for the awkward situation at Gory. Kate thought she had given the watch to Kiernan. In giving the watch to Eoin, she accepted him as her grandson.

Kate bending down on her knees to be at the same level as her mother, who was sitting on a chair. She hugged her mother, whereupon, Kate, for the first time ever, saw her mother cry.

Moments later, brushing the tears from her cheeks, Kate opened the watch and held it for Eoin to see. Kate told him, "Grandma Genevieve, who as you know is my Momma, wants you to have this very precious gift from her and my father whose name you bear. I shall keep it for you until you are old enough to receive this special inheritance."

Eoin who had been looking on at this encounter between his mother and grandmother, saw no one fall, no one was hurt, yet he saw an unusual and bewildering sight. These were tears of a different kind. It was, in fact, through their tears of joy, more than their hugs that he knew these two women loved each other. From that moment this new grandmother in his life became very special to him.

CHAPTER 11

A dark cloud of drastic change hung over the people of the lane. Conversations were saturated with unanswered questions.

The government, in its collective wisdom, or lack thereof, decided to demolish all the dwellings in the lane. In the '40s when TB was rampant, and too many people shared a bed in overcrowded living spaces, this might have been a good idea, but now in the '50s with none but two large families remaining, and TB eradicated, this action seemed an outrage to the people of the lane. All pleas to let this small community survive fell on deaf ears.

In what order would they leave? Where in Dublin would their new accommodations be? Could they still attend the church they and their families had for generations attended? How far would they be from a hospital and stores? Would any of them ever again be in walking distance of their beloved strand?

With only a few days notice, they were informed that the demolition would begin the following Monday. The three families—an elderly couple, an unmarried brother and sister, a widow and her retarded son for whom the government had found living quarters would be the first to leave.

Kate got together with the women of the lane to have a farewell party to ease the pain of their loss. They would bring all their kitchen tables and chairs and line them up in two lines, closed off at each end by table and chairs, making a large O shape. This would be done approximately a half an hour before the meal would be brought out.

Kate bought legs of lamb and a large goose, which the women cooked along with potatoes, turnips, stuffing, and gravy from both meats. Kate made a trifle with enough sherry in it to blunt what they were forced to prepare for and leave a happy memory of their time together in the lane.

It was a year after Genevieve McCormack's visit and an appropriate time for such an event—October, a time when the hard work of gathering the harvest is completed and celebrated in farmhouses across the country. The weather had been beautiful for several days, and the sun shone down on them on Sunday morning a few hours before the noontime meal.

Everyone was in great spirits, as though they had not a care in the world. Dermot Donovan played his fiddle while waiting for the meal to be put on the tables. The meat was carved and piled onto platters, bowls of potatoes and turnips were brought to the tables, and each person brought their own cutlery, plate, cup and saucer as all dwellers of the lane sat down together for their first and last time. To the surprise of all, O'Toole, having accepted Kate's invitation, sat down beside young Eoin and Kate to join his fellow neighbors for the feast.

"It's a 'bring your own poison.'" Kate had told O'Toole, who nodded in response.

By the amount of bottles on the tables that day, Kate figured each man brought enough for himself and his wife, and also enough to keep a couple of neighbors well supplied throughout the day. Much laughter and merriment accompanied the meal. Tomorrow would have its cares and woes; this day was meant for happiness.

As the meal wound down, the remaining meat was removed from the table, and a gentle rain fell—a misty rain, in which one could visualize chanting Druids of old walking. No one left the table. The women poured the tea, and the people covered it with their saucers until they were ready to drink it. The story telling continued, as did the joke telling. Peg's husband said the government probably sent the rain to let the lane people know they meant business.

"If they sent it, it wouldn't be a soft rain such as this, but a soaking with thunder and lighting," Lil answered.

Dermot took up his fiddle again and began to play as his next door neighbor held an umbrella over his instrument. Not being able to resist, people got up from the table and danced around the large O shape, laughing as they held each other's wet hands and wet clothing. Eoin O'Toole asked Kate to dance, and she was pleasantly surprised to discover how exceptionally well he moved.

A meal that began at noon continued to four o'clock, when cake and more tea was served before each family gathered their belongings and headed toward their own cottage. As the party came to a close, the people praised the gathering and the women who put it together. As the women wrapped the remaining meat, vegetables, and dessert for the first families to leave to take to their new homes, the men carried the tables indoors, and then proceeded to sweep the entire lane. It was, indeed, a beautiful memory that would live on for all of them.

In the days, weeks and months ahead, people walked back and forth from their home helping each other pack belongings and sympathizing with those most distressed by relocation.

In the chaos and lamentations of moving, Eoin O'Toole could safely visit Kate without bringing attention to himself, or raising questions about why this recluse entered Kate's home and hers alone.

"Will you go to live with your brother and his wife?" Kate asked.

"If at all possible, no. Not that they're not good people. They're the very best. But I feel like an embarrassment to them."

"Aw, I know that feeling," Kate replied, as she put the kettle on for tea.

"Where will you and the boy go?"

"I'm considering Dalkey. I saw a house there I'd like to put a down payment on from the money my Dad left me."

"Why Dalkey?"

"I've taken Eoin many times to Dun Laoghaire. He loves to watch the sailboats which are a beautiful sight. But what I admired was the view from Dalkey station. One day while going to Dun Laoghaire, I decided to stay on the train until Dalkey came into view, promising Eoin we'd see his beloved sailboats and ferry boats leaving from and returning to Ireland after I looked around a bit. We climbed Dalkey Hill. From the top of the hill, I looked down. What a magnificent sight. As this luscious green hill descended, it met with the railroad station. On the other side of the station was the strand, beautiful golden sand, and beyond it the sea as far as the eyes could see. I fell in love with this place."

"Would I be intruding in your life, if I took a room close by so that I will, on occasion, be able to see you and the boy?"

"It would be lovely to have you close by. Eoin and I are both very fond of you. But why take a room in a rooming house when you could come and live with us. The house I'm hoping to buy has three bedrooms. Eoin and I will each have a room, and you could use the other bedroom."

"When Francis returns you may have another child, perhaps a daughter who would be in need of a room."

"There's a nice size garden in front, and there's a quite large back yard in back of the house on which an extension could be built if extra rooms are needed."

"You've really thought ahead."

"A house is a big commitment. I want to make sure it fills our needs now and into the future, whatever that brings with it."

"Francis made a great choice when he married you, and as much as I love him, I'm angry with him for leaving you and the child. I'd like to have him tracked down, and determine what his intentions are to you both."

"No, Mr. O'Toole. Please do not track him down. It he comes back it must be of his own free will. I won't have it any other way."

"As you wish Kate, it shall be."

Having made the tea, she left it to brew for a few moments.

"I've become very attached to this cottage, this community of kind people. I may have a grander place to live, but this community will always be a very special place to me."

"And me," O'Toole agreed.

"What does your brother think of all this?"

"I hate to say it, Kate, but he sides with the government and believes these cottages should have been torn down years ago. 'Progress,' in this instant, is merely a fancy word given to a lamentable deed."

"We can't expect people outside of this small community to understand what it has meant to us."

"Well, I'm glad you are moving no further away from here than Dalkey."

"Yes, so am I. It's just a short train ride from here."

"Which of our writers are associated with Dalkey?" O'Toole asked.

"Joyce, then an unknown, taught school there, but the Martello Tower in Sandycove, a few stations closer to the city than Dalkey, is what people think of in association with Joyce."

"Yes, yet he spent but a week there."

"Yes, but the time spent there has gone down in literary history in the opening pages of *Ulysses*."

"You're right there, Kate. That man showed all our faults but none of our good qualities. How could he be so unkind to his own people?" he asked shaking his head.

"His own people weren't very kind to him. Henrik Ibsen, who was considered quite radical in his day, influenced Joyce. Ibsen, in his writings, held a mirror up to the Norwegians that they might see their faults and consider changing the status quo."

"Kate, that wasn't a mirror Joyce held up to the Irish; it was a blooming magnifying glass."

Kate laughed.

"How did the Norwegians react to Ibsen's writings?"

"His plays didn't have quite the same effect on them. Some did not like them, but the Norwegians apparently were more secure in who they were than the Irish at that time."

"In what way?"

"Norway was a free country, a free people. Under England's rule, the Irish were less than second-class citizens in their own country. They were looking for a savior, a deliverer, only to find their world-renowned citizen wrote not of their heroic past deeds or the injustice of that day, but rather blamed the victims for their own bondage."

They sat in silence for a while, drinking their tea.

"Have some bread. I made it this morning, and it's still warm."

"Still warm is it? I remember my mother's bread, hot from the oven with lots of creamery butter melting into it. How I loved the taste of Mother's bread."

"Help yourself while I pour us a second cup of tea."

As the government relocated groups of lane people, they demolished their homes so that they could not, if dissatisfied with their new dwellings, return to their former homes. Some were persuaded by their kin to live with their married children.

Unfortunately, of all that were relocated, none were in walking distance of each other. The people were provided with 'bed-sitters,' which were one-room flats of bedroom and sitting room combined with a small alcove for cooking. They also included a bathroom. Of all the people resettled, only the brother and sister were satisfied with their new arrangement. Although they dreadfully missed the people of the lane and felt like strangers in their new neighborhood, their flat was similar to the others in footage. However, not being husband and wife, they were provided with a small bedroom and bedroom/sitting room. But what they liked most was being on the ground floor, which gave them a small patch of garden that came with the flat. They enjoyed planting and seeing the results of their labor. When the brother died, his sister was alone. Not well enough to make a trip to her closest neighbor from the lane, which would entail two buses in each direction, she rarely left the flat except for church on Sunday and to purchase the few groceries. Shortly thereafter, she began to lose track of time. The streets grew more unfamiliar to her, as did her own flat, until she forgot who she was, and thus became completely lost.

Genevieve held onto the possibility that Kate, having to move in the New Year, might relocate in Gory. Alas, it was not to be. Neither would Kate be going to Gory for Christmas, but to the farm where she and the child spent their holidays.

Eoin told Ned and Mary that his other grandmother, Genevieve, wished he and his mother would go to Gory and join the McCormack family for Christmas dinner. Ned and Mary, not wishing to separate Eoin and Kate from either family, extended an invitation to Genevieve, her sons and their families, to come for Christmas dinner at the farm. They were welcome to stay as many days as they wished, and all meals would be provided during their stay. However, since the farmhouse was too small to provide sleeping accommodation, they would need to book into the hotel in the town.

Rory, Gwen, and Genevieve accepted the invitation and arrived at the Egan farm on Christmas Eve, about an hour after Kate and Eoin. Kieran and his family sent their regrets. Mary's warmth and cheerfulness made the dubious Genevieve feel very welcome, and they became good friends. Eoin showed his Grandma Genevieve around the farm and introduced her to his pony.

Looking at her son, Kate noticed how Eoin gravitated towards Rory whom he stood beside as they sang during midnight mass on Christmas Eve. He basked in his uncle's words and delighted in his humor. Although Eoin had two grandfathers who loved him, Kate realized how much her son craved a father in these growing years.

When Francis returns, what will life be like? When he left, he left a terrible void in my life. His love was freely given, only to be abruptly snatched away. That intense hurt, which she had thought would remain with her forever, had to some degree faded in the everyday tasks, difficulties, and joys of living. Knowing she was not the same person she once was caused her to wonder in what way would Francis have changed.

After mass, Eoin proudly introduced his uncle to the celebrant as they walked out of the church into the night air.

Kate wished to know where the extra horse came from. Ned explained that since she had mentioned that her brother rode, and the only riding horse on the farm was Roan, Francis' horse now ridden by Kate, he borrowed a horse from a friend's farm seven miles away. Rory and Kate rode out together into the brisk air on Christmas morning. Gwen, who did not ride, helped the women prepare breakfast.

"This is a wonderful place," Rory said, as he and Kate rubbed down the horses. "So many other things went wrong in your life."

"Yes, Rory, and so many truly lovely things entered it."

Mary served goose and ham from their farm and their own creamery butter. Both red and white wine was served with the meal, followed by Christmas pudding, which was a delight to all when the brandy was poured on top and lit. Tea and brandy accompanied thick slices of the rich dark Christmas pudding as a most fitting ending to a sumptuous meal.

Kate wondered how Francis would spend Christmas. She hoped he was with friends at this special time of year. The old year was ending and another would soon begin. *Will this be the year Francis will return home? What exactly would need to happen to bring him home?*

As they sat around the fire in the living room, each family got to know each other through conversations and remembrances. Then the singing began. Eoin was the first to sing. Ned said he did not sing but would recite Yeat's poem, "The Lake Isle of Inisfree," which he executed flawlessly and with intensity. Mary had a beautiful, soft sweet voice. Gwen and Rory did a hilarious song together which had everyone laughing. Then they urged all to join in the chorus, which they did with great gusto. Nobody wanted to call it a day, and so the evening became night, followed by morning before they retired to their beds.

CHAPTER 12

It took a year and a half to resettle all the lane people. Kate Egan and Eoin O'Toole, who had a house to move into, chose to stay in the lane until all the elderly, especially those whose children were in "far away lands," as the older people called any country further than the British Isles, were resettled. Eoin O'Toole saw to it that their old age pensions were transferred to the post offices nearest their new homes. Eoin and Kate walked with them to the post office, introduced them and inquired on what day their pension money could be collected. Then they would take them to the parish church, obtain its mass schedule, and information on other services and activities. After locating the apothecary, the hospital, the greengrocers, and other shops within easy walking distance, Eoin and Kate treated the older people to lunch before returning with them to their new accommodations. Then they bade them goodbye and wished them happiness in their new homes.

All the women who had banded together when anyone was in need—Liz, Siobhan, Monica, Kathleen, Tara, Peg, and Kate—agreed to get together for a day, once a year.

"That makes parting a bit easier," Tara said holding back the tears as each one of them left. They hugged and wept in each other's arms.

"God forgive them," Kathleen said as she left the lane.

Some turned back to wave and take a last look, but others could not look back at the devastation of the only home they, their parents, and grandparents had ever known. Who they were as a people was being buried in the rubble.

At age six and one half, Eoin Egan was a happy boy. He made friends easily, and his passions were hurling and soccer, both of which he played at school. The strand was just downhill from his new home. Unlike the adults, Eoin was not burdened with feelings of loss on leaving the lane, and instead delighted in his new surroundings.

As Eoin and his friends walked home from school on a beautiful autumn day, they kicked the leaves from the curb and watched them fly into the air, as they talked of Hallows Eve, just a fortnight away. Eoin also looked forward to his birthday at the end of November when he would become seven years old.

Their frolicking came to a sudden stop as a car pulled up to the curb.

"Eoin Egan," a man seated in the back seat called out as he lowered the window.

Eoin, astonished that a person he'd never before met, knew his name, stopped. The man opened the car door.

"You lads can walk on. I just wish to speak to Eoin." The man's voice from within the car addressed the two other boys who had stopped to see what this interruption in their walk home was all about.

After a moment's hesitation, they did as the man suggested,

although one them looked back asking his friend as he did so, "Shouldn't we wait for Eoin?"

"The man knows him. Didn't he call him by name?"

"Yes, but look here, John, the man pulled Eoin into the car. Now if Eoin wanted to get in, why would the man need to pull him into the car?"

"It looked to me like Eoin got in by himself. All the man did was hold out an arm to him."

"Before you turned around, I saw him pull Eoin into the car! What if Eoin is being kidnapped?"

"You need to be rich and famous like Lindbergh before anyone would bother kidnapping a person, and I never heard of anyone being kidnapped in Ireland."

Niall saw the truth in his friend's words, and his uneasiness with what he saw, or thought he saw, faded.

Eoin's pleadings to be released so that he could return home were in vain. He recognized Dun Laoghaire harbor for his mother had many times brought him there to see the sailboats and sometimes there were larger boats docked in the harbor that transported people and their cars to England, France, Spain, and Holland. With panic of such intensity never before known to him, Eoin knew that they were about to leave Ireland.

"Where are we going?" the boy asked with fear in his voice.

As the woman drove the car onto the boat, the man warned Eoin against speaking to anybody or drawing attention to himself. If he should do so, the man said, he would never again see his mother. To further convince the boy he should do as he was told, the man mentioned his mother by name and the hospital where she worked. Eoin, who did not want anything bad to happen to his mother, obeyed this man.

Once inside the boat, they got out of the car and walked to the enclosed deck above. Very few people were on this level for it was without sun on this beautiful sunny day. The open deck above was crowded with people eating, sunning themselves, and playing cards, while children ran around in play.

Eoin wondered who the woman was who had driven the car and was now traveling with them. As though the man could read his thoughts, he said, "This here is Maude. I'm Harry, and I'm your real father."

Eoin tried hard not to think, afraid the man might read his mind again, but thoughts came regardless of how hard he tried to suppress them. He did not believe this man was his father.

Maude must be his wife, Eoin thought, and wondered why then did they not have children of their own, and let him go back to his mother. This man Harry did not look at all like his father in the picture of his father and mother on their wedding day. His mother kept it in the top drawer and told Eoin he could look at it anytime he desired to do so. Besides, his father's name was Francis Egan, and his own name was Egan. Harry did not mention his surname. Well, if he can read minds, the boy thought, maybe he'll tell me his last name.

Nothing but silence followed until Harry addressed Maude.

"Get us some beer and chips and lemonade for the lad."

"Well, aren't you going to give me the money for the beer and chips?"

"What do you do with all the money I keep handing you?"

"Do you want beer or not?"

Harry took some bills from his pocket and handed them to her.

Harry held onto the boy throughout the trip. The loving father with his arm around his son's shoulders was the pose most used. One hand on Eoin's knee while Harry ate, and at times around his waist, all of which Eoin knew was to remind him to keep quiet and not cause anyone to become suspicious.

While Maude was getting the beer and chips, a middle-aged couple walking by smiled at Eoin. Eoin's eyes implored the woman to rescue him. Instead, she asked him if he would like some chocolate. Knowing he must not speak, he nodded his head.

"Is the boy all right?" the woman asked Harry as she handed Eoin a piece of chocolate.

"Fine, why do you ask?"

"He doesn't look well," the woman answered as though trying to figure something out.

"No, it's just a touch of sea sickness he's got. He'll be as right as rain after we have landed." Harry reached over, took the chocolate from Eoin and pocketed it saying, "I'll give it to him later when he's feeling better."

The woman was very sympathetic, but of no help to Eoin who had seen the woman as his only hope of escape before landing on foreign soil. Her husband, who had not uttered a word, smiled at the boy as they walked away.

In putting the beer, lemonade and potato chips down, Maude, who had witnessed this scene from the sidelines, said in a loud whisper, "You're a smooth one, Harry Browne."

Through his downcast spirit, which covered him like a wet newspaper, Eoin heard the name. Although he never believed that Harry was his father, now he felt he had proof positive that Harry Browne had lied to him.

Half an hour before the boat arrived in port, Harry told Maude and Eoin it was time to get into the car. Sitting in the dark interior of the car, Harry asked Maude if she had a nail scissor in her handbag. Maude routed around in her handbag and drew out a small scissor.

"Cut the school emblem off his blazer pocket. We don't want anyone looking at that and wondering what school it is that he attends."

Maude carefully cut the emblem off, as the boy's eyes filled with tears, which did not fall.

"It's all right, ducks, I'll sew it back on when it's time for you to go home," Maude softly assured him on seeing the boy's distress.

Shortly, other people came down to the car level and got into their cars, preparing to leave as soon as the opening doors were lowered. *Would my mother know where to find me? Is this where my real father lives? If this was another country why did it not look different? Would people speak like Maude did, here in this place? How could I find a policeman and if I did find one, how could I speak to him with Harry ever at my side?* Eoin's thoughts were interrupted as the opening was unsealed. Soon the cars are moving off the boat. Maude drove on the boat, but it was Harry who was driving off it. They drove for quite a long time without stopping. It was dark when they came into the city of London.

"Don't you think we should get something to eat?"

"And how are we going to do that without advertising what we're up to?"

"It'll take us forty-five minutes or more to get to the flat, and there's nothing to eat when we get there."

"There's a chip shop around the corner. You'll go out and get us some food! You better watch it! Your brain is going to rust from lack of use."

"Brains cannot rust. They have no metal parts!" Eoin joined in the conversation.

"I thought you said he was asleep," Harry said under his breath.

"He was."

"We're almost there, ducky. I bet you're hungry. We'll get something to eat as soon as we reach the flat. Do you like fish and chips?"

"Yes."

"What a dumb question to ask him. Don't you think they eat fish and chips in Ireland?"

"How am I supposed to know? I was never there before this trip."

"Are you planning on sharing any more vital information?"

"Sorry."

Eoin tried to read the writing on the walls as they climbed up many stairs to the flat, but the light was very dim, and Harry walked very fast and told him to stop dawdling. Harry told Maude to pick up a newspaper when she went out for the fish and chips, and when she returned he seemed more interested in the newspaper than the food. Harry spread the newspaper on the coffee table, the only table in the flat.

Eoin, who was very hungry, ate his share of the food from the bag with his fingers while sitting on the grimy furniture in the dirtiest place Eoin had ever set foot in.

"Well?"

"Nothing yet," Harry answered.

At night when they went to bed, Harry stated that Eoin would sleep in the room with the double bed while he and Maude would take the other room with the two dilapidated single beds. Maude questioned Harry's reasoning on this but Harry ignored her. Later as he went to bed, it became clear to Maude and Eoin why Harry had come to this decision. Eoin stated that he had no pajamas to sleep in, so Harry told him to sleep in his underwear. After Eoin was in bed, Harry tied a rope from the doorknob of Eoin's room to the bathroom doorknob. The other bedroom was without a doorknob, and didn't close properly.

"Where am I going to pee during the night?" Maude asked.

"Don't know. Don't care. This bathroom is now off limits."

Eoin had been living in this filthy flat in a rather unsavory part of London for a week and lamenting every day to both Harry and Maude about missing so much school. He had asked Maude, "Why don't you and Harry get a child of your own?"

Maude laughed. Seeing the serious and confused look on the boy's face, she apologized.

"We're not married, duckie. Harry's not the marrying kind."

"If he's not married, how can he be my father?"

Maude, hearing Eoin's question, knew she had said too much, and was glad Harry was not there to hear what she had said. *This is a smart boy. I wonder what his mother is like. Harry said she was a nurse. They seemed to produce a hell of a lot of nurses in Ireland. Even in our hospitals, one is bound to run into Irish nurses.*

"He is your father. That's a fact."

"He's not married to my mother, so he cannot be my father."

"It's complicated, Eoin, and you'll figure it all out when you're older. Harry's not the most honest person, but the truth is, he is your father."

Yes, it was complicated, and he was very confused. This conversation had hit a brick wall, and his head was still spinning. Yes, too complicated.

"When do you think I can attend school? I've lost a whole week already."

"Can't tell you that, Eoin, for I don't know."

"My clothes are getting all mussed up. My shirt has lots of creases in it."

"We can't do much about your clothes, ducks."

"Harry said I'd never see Mom again if I didn't do everything he told me to do. Well, I've done everything he asked, and I'm wondering when I can see Mom again. 'She'll be worried sick,'" he added, using an expression he often heard in the lane.

Maude had no answer to give him.

He wished he were back in the lane where everyone made sure all were safe, and this kidnapping could never have happened.

CHAPTER 13

For the first time in her life, Kate found she could not function. Inconsolable, she sat in the rocking chair where she had breastfed Eoin as a baby and recalled the past almost seven years of his life. *Even before Eoin was born, Francis', Eoin's and my life were entwined. In trying to protect this unborn child, I found the courage to engage Francis, a total stranger, in conversation. It was my need to protect Eoin, even before birth, that brought us together. It was also my misdeed that put him in danger. Would Harry actually harm Eoin? Harry was furious with me for preventing him from taking Eoin in order to save his marriage to Kit. But would he hurt our son? No, he had many faults, but I doubt that he would intentionally bring harm to Eoin. I pray I'm not wrong in this.*

The Garda entered her home after Eoin O'Toole responded to their knocking on the door.

"We're sorry for your troubles," the older of the Garda said as he drew close to the rocking chair.

"Thank you," she answered in a barely audible voice.

"I gather your son was wearing his school uniform the day he disappeared?" the Garda asked.

"Yes. Navy blue blazer with the school crest on the pocket, gray flannel pants, and blue shirt with a navy and blue striped tie."

"Did anyone see this happen? Children usually walk home from school in small groups. Who would have walked with your son?"

"He walked home with John and Niall. They are neighboring boys. They're older than Eoin, about nine and ten years old."

"Good. They should be old enough to give a good description of anyone who might have talked to them or what might have enticed Eoin to go with this person, and if this person had an accomplice. Where can we find these two lads?"

Kate directed the Garda to the boys' homes.

"We'll need to talk to you again, Mrs. Egan," the younger man said although he had remained silent while the other had done all the talking.

"Will tomorrow morning at ten o'clock be all right with you?"

Kate nodded her head.

The Garda questioned Niall Dempsey in his home. Niall believed Eoin was forced into a car. "The man knew Eoin's name," Niall told the Garda.

"Did he call Eoin by his first or last name?"

"Both. He called to him from the car."

"A car?"

"Yes, sir."

"What kind of a car?"

"Don't know, sir."

"What else did this man say?"

"He told us to walk on. He wanted to talk to Eoin."

"Did he say anything else?"

"No, sir."

"Can you give us a description of this man?"

"He had dark hair. He looked like he had a suntan."

"Did he have an Irish or English accent, or might he have had a foreign one?"

After a pause the boy answered.

"I think it was a bit like an Irish accent and a bit like an English one."

"Was the man sitting in the driver's seat?"

"He was sitting in the back seat."

"What did the person who was sitting in the driver's seat look like?"

"Don't know, sir."

"Was it a man or a woman?"

"Don't know, sir."

"Can you think of anything else that happened or was said at that time?"

"No, sir."

"You've done very well, Niall, and we appreciate your help. If you can think of anything else, no matter how insignificant it may appear, call us at this number.

The Garda handed Niall a card with a telephone number on it, which made the boy feel very important and very willing to do all the Garda required of him.

John Hughes' story was somewhat different, but most helpful in that the boys recalled different details. John thought Eoin was helped into the car, but he had not looked back until after Niall believed he saw Eoin being forced into the car. When asked who was driving the car, Niall had no idea while John said it was a woman. Yes, he was sure of that. John described the woman as having frizzy, blonde hair, like a bad permanent. One of John's sisters had a friend who had such a permanent, so he knew of these things. The woman had fair skin, and from what he saw of her face and shoulders, he believed she was a bit on the heavy side. Neither of the boys could describe any facial features of either the man or the woman. John was also given a card with a telephone number and asked to call if he remembered any other details.

When the Garda returned the following morning, they asked the question that would cause Kate the most trouble, and would be the most important information in this case. After a few minutes of greetings, offering and declining tea, apologies for intruding again at this agonizing time in her life, the question was asked.

"Do you know, Mrs. Egan, anyone who might want to hurt the child or you? Anyone from your past who might hold a grievance against you?"

Yes, I do. Kate knew it had to be him. *Harry had tried to take the boy before but he was no longer married to Kit Fitzgerald. Why now? And for what purpose?* She wondered.

"There is someone who might have a motive. His name is Harry Browne."

"Where can we find this Harry Browne?"

"I don't know. The last time I heard of him he was married to Brian Fitzgerald's daughter. But they have since had the marriage annulled."

"This Brian Fitzgerald you speak of, is he the Brian Fitzgerald who owns the racehorse facilities in Kildare?"

"Yes."

"Who is this Mr. Browne in relationship to you?"

"He is Eoin's biological father who left me as soon as he learned I was pregnant."

"Are you now or were you ever married to Harry Browne?"

"We did not marry."

"When was the last time you saw him?"

"He came to the cottage I was living in before I moved here. It was about five years ago. He and his wife couldn't conceive a child, and he offered me money in exchange for Eoin. When I refused, he threatened to take me to court to gain custody of Eoin. When he found his case against me was too weak, he dropped it."

"And you haven't seen him since?"

"I have not seen him since."

"That sheds light on this case." The detective reflected on this a moment. "If it were Browne, he would, of course, know the boy's name."

Eoin O'Toole asked the Garda to keep Kate's past indiscretions from the newspapers. Not being able to get a positive answer to his request from the Garda, he phoned his brother, explained the situation and asked for his brother's help.

"Why is it that your every request is to help others? This woman is married. Her relationships are a mess. She had a child by one man and married another, and both men left her! Why do you get involved with people like her? What kind of hold does this Kate Egan have on you, Eoin?"

"That most difficult kind, I love her. No, don't go off into absurd thinking. She's like a daughter to me. This may not be the best time to tell you this, but I'm the father of the husband who left her, which makes Kate my daughter-in-law."

A moment of silence followed.

"Eoin, you never married."

"True. I did, however, have a child."

"My God, Eoin, this is no time to joke."

"It certainly isn't."

Another loud but brief silence followed.

"Does she know you're her father-in-law?"

"Yes. We are aware of our unsavory pasts. She has asked only for help regarding her small son. She's spent the last seven years protecting her child, and now this has happened. The past, which we thought she had left behind her, has erupted to destroy her life and put her son's life in jeopardy. Can you keep this out of the newspapers for Kate's and the boy's sake?"

"I'm a judge, Eoin. This is out of my jurisdiction. I'll see what I can do, but I can't promise you I can stop the newspapers printing her past indiscretions. This kind of thing is their cup of tea."

"Thanks."

"Eoin, why didn't you tell me about your son?"

"You were a promising young lawyer who at a young age became a judge. I was a lovesick young man who wanted to give the object of my love the one thing her happy marriage did not produce, a child. Back then only the child's mother and I knew. Aoife died when the child was eleven years old."

"Aoife! I remember your being head over heels in love with her. Beautiful Aoife! I gather her husband thought the child was his?

"He believed it was his child. It had to be that way. I had no claim on the child. Kate and I are the only ones who know. Now you, too, know."

"The young man, does he not know?"

"He does not."

"Don't you think you should tell him?"

"I will."

Judge O'Toole, after getting through to Detective Keegan, was infuriated by this man's wandering on about the media's need to know, and how withholding some information on this case might hamper the rescue of this boy.

"What I ask, Detective, is that you cut it short. I do not ask that you hold back any vital information; just the titillating stuff."

"That's what sells newspapers."

"The mother of the kidnapped boy is married to a man other than the boy's father. This woman has just had her son kidnapped. It would be damnable cruel to add more grief to her lot, don't you agree, Detective?"

Not receiving an immediate response from the detective, the judge continued.

"Do you have a wife, Detective, and children?"

"Yes to both."

"How old are the children?"

"Seven and ten years old."

"Your seven-year-old is just a few months older than the kidnapped boy. You'd want your child back if he was kidnapped, and you'd also want to spare his distraught mother any additional distress. Is that not true?"

"True. But I have no control over the press."

"All I ask is that you give them the necessary information without destroying anyone's reputation in the process."

Detective Keegan was in a difficult spot. This happened in his precinct. The reporters would want to know why he had not given them the full scoop. He needed the press to give his men favorable reports, to play up their good work and citations received, and downplay some of the fumbling and happenings that might be a bit of an embarrassment to the Garda. Now this judge wanted to destroy his rapport with the press.

Why? What has this mother and son got to do with Judge O'Toole? I could put that bright new recruit on this, and see what he can find!

Brian Fitzgerald read of the kidnapping in the evening newspaper, and immediately phoned Kate. Eoin O'Toole answered the telephone. When Fitzgerald asked what he could do to help Kate, O'Toole voiced his concerns. Fitzgerald, who was greatly distressed by the child's abduction, spoke of his annoyance when Browne tried to reclaim the child he abandoned and present him as his grandchild. When, by accident, he met young Eoin at the Dublin Horse Show, he wished the child were his grandson. Then he saw Kate, a young woman about his daughter's age, and he hated Harry Browne for doing so much harm to both these fine women. His daughter had remarried and was very happy. He was very angry to discover that Browne was still making trouble for Kate, and pledged to do all in his power to help in the return of the boy and keep Browne from interfering in their lives. It would be Fitzgerald who would see to it that the story was told without its more private and personal aspects coming to light.

Eoin had a question to ask Harry, and it had been floating around in his head for a few days while he waited patiently for the right moment to approach him. Harry was quite erratic and prone to sudden eruptions of anger. He did not go to work each morning and return in the evening, Eoin noted. In fact, it did not seem to the boy that Harry had any set time to do anything, not even to eat. Maude also did not know when Harry might leave or return.

Eoin liked Maude. She was fat and jolly. She was a fun sort of person when Harry wasn't around. She spoke to him as another individual, whereas Harry, in the rare times he spoke to him, treated Eoin as something between a troublesome child and a family pet. Harry did, however, when speaking to him, refer to him as 'son.' It was this that got the boy thinking.

Harry came home, and without a word to Maude or Eoin, sat down in the soiled, overstuffed armchair and turned on the radio. With his right hand he set about checking all the news stations, and with the bent fingers of his left hand, he tapped in a continuous Morse code-like fashion on the armrest.

No, this did not appear to be the right moment to ask Harry the question I have in mind, Eoin thought. Maud had a few questions of her own to ask, but she too waited.

"Did you cook us anything?" Harry broke his concentration to ask about a half an hour after he had sat down.

"You didn't leave any money."

"If I gave you a twenty and you bought something for five, the very next time you'd ask again for money. What about my change?"

"Didn't know you wanted the change! Didn't know you were that cheap!"

"Now I know why some husbands strangle wives."

"Well, that excludes us, now, doesn't it?"

"Here take this ten and get us some fish and chips," Harry stated, taking the money from his pants pocket and throwing it on the stool in front of him.

"I hope this covers it."

"Make it."

Maude picked up the money.

"Do you want to come with me, Eoin?"

"Are you mad, woman?"

"It's already dark out. That child hadn't been outside this stinking flat since we got here. He gets no fresh air. He's liable to get sick, and then you'll have real worries, Harry."

"I'll take him out for a walk when I have time."

"Yeah, when pigs fly," Maud retorted and slammed the door on the way out.

Harry was angry. Maude had given him something to worry about, and he did not like to think about worrisome things. His left hand had stopped beating out its coded message. Harry began to hit his fist into his open hand while remaining silent for what seemed to Eoin a long time. After a little while, Harry returned to browsing through the stations again. Finding a station that he liked, Harry sat back in the armchair and smiled, which was the closest he came to contentment.

"Harry?"

Harry looked at the boy in surprise.

"What is it, son?"

"If you are my real father, you would want me to go to school and learn."

Harry stared at the boy, while Eoin wondered what Harry would do.

"Boys are not supposed to like school."

"But, I do, sir. I like it a lot."

"Why?"

"I like to learn new things, and I like playing hurling and soccer with my school mates."

"Well, they don't play hurling here. They play some stupid thing called cricket."

"Then I could learn to play cricket," the boy answered with joy bursting out on his face.

Harry, who considered children to be noisy, pestering, demanding little people, never had wanted a child of his own, except to win over Fitzgerald. He looked at this child, who but for his mother's integrity, would not have been born, and found that he liked Eoin. He liked him a lot.

Would I have been more like him if I didn't grow up dirt poor; if I went to a better school; if anyone cared a damn if I learned anything or not; if my old man could have kept a job?

He could not promise his son that he could go to school, because they would be only temporarily at this location. They could not stay in London. Harry had planned to be in Spain by now, but insufficient funds caused a delay. The bookie was late in paying him his winnings. *The bookie's father died at a hell of an inconvenient time,* Harry thought. When they reached Spain they would settle down and the boy could attend school.

It's his mother's fault. That bitch ruined my marriage to Kit and caused Fitzgerald to become my enemy, and he's too powerful a man to have as an enemy. She probably thought that whole ugliness was over and done with. Nobody takes Harry Browne over the coals and gets away with it.

How could she have retained the best legal minds in Dublin? She had an inheritance! Probably one of those trusts held until the child is twenty-one, twenty-five, or thirty years old. Of all the women I've been with, it is Kate I should have married. Of course, I would have had to change my lifestyle, cut out gambling and women, and gotten a decent job. Her inheritance would have cushioned things. Her father or grandfather, whoever decided she would have to wait for her inheritance until she was older and wiser, did her a favor, and me a disfavor.

Egan could not stomach the fact that Eoin was my son, and walked away from the best deal he could ever get in this life.

I was only planning on keeping the lad for a few weeks to let her feel the pain. All her past will be exposed. She'll be notorious. The papers will have a field day with the respectable Kate Egan's past. She'll soon know that even with her money and fancy lawyers, she can't get the best of Harry. He's my son! I too have a claim on him. I can keep the lad away from my occupations. I might even keep him. He's almost seven. He'll be easy to take care of, and maybe we'll become friends! Harry smiled at the possibility.

I had to fight for everything I got. How did Kate, who grew up without want and attended the best schools, become such a fighter, a worthy opponent of old Harry? I hated her for it, and yet was overwhelmed by that opposite feeling, which I tried to ignore. Can a person hate someone and at the same time love that someone? Nobody ever brought out such strong feeling in me as Kate. Damn you, Kate McCormack.

I was too young. I wasn't ready for marriage, and definitely not ready for a child. I was going to make my fortune! I was going to have it all. Alas, I didn't recognize my good fortune when it fell into my lap. Even without her money, she was the prize.

The Dublin Garda contacted the British police who were now trying to locate both Harry Browne and Francis Egan in connection with the kidnapping of Eoin Egan. When contacted, Brian Fitzgerald gave a very damaging character reference of Harry Browne.

Friends had come with cheerful words about the child they expected to soon be reunited with his mother and family. They had brought food and flowers. After the many visitors had left, Eoin O'Toole said "He was safe in the lane," as he sat by the fire across from Kate late in the evening.

"I was just thinking the same thing," Kate answered.

"This Browne, what kind of fellow is he?"

"He's a charming rogue. A gambler, womanizer, and not someone one could oppose without paying dearly."

"Might he harm the child?"

"He a very unsavory person, yet I don't believe he'd harm my son or any child."

"That's good to know."

"No guarantees comes with that."

"Understood. You've got to get some sleep," he told the exhausted

Kate, but sleep ignored her and would not come. "There'll be another stream of people here tomorrow."

"We've told the police everything, several times over," the weary woman sighed, "yet they still come to ask questions. Thank you, Eoin, for being a buffer between me, the police, and reporters."

"I'll fix us some cocoa, and then it's to bed," Eoin said on rising.

Rory and Gwen insisted on taking Eoin O'Toole and Kate out to various locations for dinner during their visit in support for Kate. Both Eoin and Kate enjoyed their company, and found they could leave their deepest pain behind them at these times. Genevieve McCormack, tired of traveling back and forth to her daughter's home, decided to take up residence in young Eoin's room until her much prayed-for grandson would be returned. Genevieve joined the foursome for dinner one evening, and Kieran and his wife arrived at Dalkey to offer whatever help they could during the two days they spent there.

It was not until a group of women from the lane showed up at the house that Kate cried, releasing the pain that weighed heavily on her as she was being warmly hugged by each one of them. That night Kate slept the night through. These women hadn't been afraid to mention Eoin's name. In fact they recalled his birth in the cottage, and how efficient and brave Kate had been. Eoin's Hallows' Eve outfits caused much laughter among them, and on and on they related events right up to and including the great outdoor meal and dancing around the tables in the rain.

Genevieve thought this might upset Kate; it was too reminiscent of a wake, but Kate and Eoin O'Toole enjoyed reliving these times. The reserved Genevieve had a difficult time getting used to the familiarity of this group of women. Yet, when she saw the comfort they gave her daughter and the kind Mr. O'Toole, Genevieve appreciated their presence. Rory and Gwen enjoyed meeting and conversing with those they referred to as "Kate's good friends from the lane," and the lane friends were delighted with Rory and Gwen.

"He'll be back, Kate," Monica said. "It's just the waiting that's harrowing."

"How can he not come home? The churches are all praying for his safe return as are all the children at school," Tara said.

"We've even got our husbands and their friends from work attending mass at noon," Peg declared. "Now as soon as God recovers from the shock of seeing them all at the noontime mass, he's bound to see that Eoin is safely returned."

Kidnapped! It sounded so horrible. Genevieve recalled the turmoil and stresses an aviator and his wife endured when their son was kidnapped. They paid the ransom, but whether by intent or accident, the child had died. That thought sent a chill through Genevieve's slight frame. The Garda asked if there was a ransom note, but Kate had received none.

CHAPTER 14

On a Sunday morning, Eoin O'Toole answered the phone, which was his custom to keep unwanted calls from Kate.

"Good morning."

"Good morning to you. Have I got the correct number for Kate Egan?"

"Yes. Who is calling?"

"Francis Egan."

Eoin could not speak for a few seconds.

"Are you still there?" the caller asked.

"Yes, Francis, this is Eoin O'Toole. How are you, son?" Eoin asked in a manner often used by an older man to a younger one, whether related or not.

"I heard on the news about young Eoin being abducted. How dreadful. Kate must be beside herself with grief. The police were looking for Harry Browne and me, so I went to the police station and identified myself. They wanted to know if I knew where Browne was, but of course, I don't. I hadn't known he was in England. So I gather they haven't found him yet. Three hours later, after a flood of questions and much waiting around, they released me, saying I'm to keep myself available for further questioning. So I must stay in the vicinity until this terrible thing is settled."

"It's so good, Francis, to hear your voice again. But it is Kate you want to speak to, and she you, so I'll give her a shout. God bless you."

At the sound of her name, Kate came in from the kitchen and softly asked, "Who is it?"

Eoin handed her the phone without answering her question.

"Good morning."

"Good morning, Kate." Kate reached out and lowered herself into a nearby chair. "I heard about young Eoin, and I'm dreadfully sorry. How are you holding up under the strain?"

"With difficulty."

"The police have questioned me, and inform me I can't leave the country, actually not even the precinct as they might want to question me again. As soon as they clear me, I'll return to Dublin." After a brief pause he added, "That's if it's all right with you."

"Yes, of course. Ned and Mary will be delighted to see you." After she had said that, she regretted it. She hadn't known a residue of pain at his leaving still lay within her. She was about to amend her statement by adding that she, too, would be happy to see him, when he spoke.

"I'd like very much to see you, Kate."

"Let me give you my address."

The operator was asking for more coins. Kate recalled her phone calls to Kieran and the constant need, while using the public phone booth, for more coins.

"I've got a fist full of shillings, six-penny, and three-penny pieces," Francis assured her, "and also a pencil here with me."

He took down her address and then asked, "Eoin O'Toole answered your phone. How did you get a recluse such as him to visit you?"

Kate told him of the government's edict, the destruction of the cottages, and that Eoin O'Toole was not visiting, but living with them.

"Mr. O'Toole would be delighted to see you come home"

"Apparently I have no home to come home to!"

"Yes, you do." She did not elaborate further.

"I'll be back as soon as I am permitted to leave England. It's been great hearing your voice again."

"Hearing yours has been a lovely surprise and at a time when I needed something good to happen. God be with you."

"And with you, Kate."

Kate hung up the phone.

If it's been so great hearing my voice, why then didn't he call sooner? It took the kidnapping of my son to trigger this call. It's been over seven years since we married. After seven years of separation, are we still legally married? Will we be strangers to one another? How does one start over again? Will this anger of mine that has resurfaced destroy any chance we have as a couple, as a family?

Eoin has no memory of Francis. How will he react? What if he feels this man, from a wedding photograph, is an intruder in our lives? What if Eoin is never found? Banish that thought, she demanded of herself.

Kate was both happy and angry with Francis. When she shared with Eoin O'Toole how she felt, he said, "His call was a temporary relief from the strain of Eoin being missing. That is good. You needed a diversion from that, and this combination of happiness and anger is just the thing."

"Eoin, how can I go back to a man who has not forgiven an earlier transgression? I treated Francis very shabbily. I tried to pass off Harry's child as his. I have always believed, and have no reason to believe otherwise now, that Francis never forgave me, and that was why he left, not to return. That's a long time to hold back forgiveness. 'Twas a terrible start to a marriage, and that was my fault. Francis would not discuss the matter. His solution was to leave. I believe Harry was the force behind this kidnapping, and this action on Harry's part was what prompted Francis to telephone me. Isn't that a strange twist of fate?"

"Yes, indeed. Don't make any assumptions or decisions, Kate, until you've had an opportunity for a long talk with Francis."

Kate nodded in agreement.

Everyone knew Harry Browne, the police discovered, but nobody knew where he was. Harry kept himself hidden until he received his winnings from the betting shop. All he had to do now was take the boy, give Maude the slip, and leave London. Everything was going his way, he thought, as he returned to the furnished flat. But when he got there, he was greeted by disarray. The boy was missing, and according to the words written on the bathroom mirror, he was being held as a hostage as part of an honor killing. Apparently, the beautiful Indian maiden Harry had had sex with was pregnant. The brothers and uncles of the woman planned to murder her and kill Harry. Since Harry wasn't home, they took his son. His son would be spared if Harry came forward. Maude, who went into hiding after the intruders left, returned when she saw Harry. They had asked her if the boy was Harry's son, and she had said, "Yes."

"Did you phone the police?"

"No, they told me they would kill the boy if I did and then come back and kill me. They had long knives hidden in their clothes. Are you going to tell the police?"

"Are you stupid, woman? What did they tell you would happen if you told the police?"

Maude began to repeat what she had just told Harry, but he cut her short.

"Shut up, woman," Harry angrily told her.

"I need a go-between," Harry, said as if speaking to himself.

"Not me," the frightened woman said.

"No, definitely not you. I need someone with a functioning brain. The bookie! I've got make some phone calls."

These people work fast. They won't wait. I've got to make a deal with them. Harry phoned his bookie, and then phoned the number the intruders had taped unto the bathroom mirror. He then packed a bag.

"I've got to pay someone a visit."

"Don't leave me. They might come back." Harry ignored her. "Is Eoin safe?"

"I'm reasonably sure he is . . . for now."

"Harry, what should we do?"

Addressing the woman he answered, "We? You stay here. In a little less than an hour, you can turn on the evening news and find out if I have escaped or my blood is congealing in a nasty stain in a men's room at Victoria Station." As he zippered up the leather jacket he had not taken off since he came into the flat, he continued, "After the news, leave here immediately. Go home or stay with friends," he added, and closing the door behind him, he left.

I don't want to bloody well die. I don't want anything to happen to the kid. I wish I had never claimed him as my son. This has got to be the worse predicament I've ever gotten into. I'm a pro at getting out of trouble, but this honor thing means death. If I don't show up, they'll kill the boy, which may not prevent them from eventually coming after me. Which is it to be?

Maude, paralyzed by indecision, thought. *Harry doesn't have a prayer in hell of outwitting anyone when they want revenge. Harry said I should stay here, but if they kill Harry and the boy, they'll surely come for me. They don't know I can't tell the differences between Indian and Pakistani, only that I am the person that may be able to tie the killings to them. I've got to leave right away.*

Maude was in the process of putting her few belongings in a bag when she heard a knock on the door. It's them, she thought. They've come to cut my throat! Drowning in fear, her knees buckled, and she slid to the floor. As she was recovering, she heard a voice on the other side of the door.

"This is the police. Open the door." What the two policemen found was a hysterical woman bubbling about throats being cut and an innocent boy.

"Where is Harry Browne?"

"He'd kill me if I spoke to the police."

"Harry is in real trouble. There's little we can do for him, but we might be able to save the boy. If you don't want this child murdered, you will tell us where this meeting is to take place!"

"Victoria Station."

"Where in the station?" the police officer asked. Maude was drawing a blank. Too much had happened in such a short time span. "Get out of here and find some safe place," they told Maude as they rushed from the building into the waiting police car. Once inside the car, one of the men put on the siren while pressing his foot down on the petrol pedal. The other policeman phoned into the station.

Harry had insisted on being able to see the boy. When he had asked for assurance that they would not harm the boy if he showed up in his stead, he was told he had their word on it, and added their word was their bond.

"You can murder a female relative and another person in cold blood and speak of honor!? Harry had questioned.

"A man without honor cannot understand the weight of honor," they had gently assured him, as though they were sorry for this deficiency in him.

Harry, disguised in a hat and coat he had gotten from a charity shop, was wearing glasses as he walked to the designated bathroom with the out-of-order sign hanging from the door. He had not prayed since he was a boy, and his mind fumbled for a familiar prayer from his youth. All he could come up with was a night prayer. "Here I lay me down to sleep, I pray the Lord my soul to keep, and if I die . . . ," Harry gulped, and with courage he did not possess, opened the door and walked in.

Eoin, wearing a white tunic, was standing just inside the entrance to the bathroom between two young men still in their teens. At the opposite end, smiling as though this was a dignified business affair, were four men waiting for Harry. Two stepped forward and proceeded to take Harry to the far end of the restroom.

Eoin, on seeing Harry, called out to him.

Harry addressed the boy.

"You'll be going home to your mom, now. I lied. I'm not your father, but I couldn't want for a finer young man as a son than you. Safe home, Eoin." Harry could not understand their strange code of conduct but felt they would keep their word and release his son.

One of the young men standing next to Eoin immediately stood in front of him, blocking his view of Harry, while the other young man moved behind the boy and held his head firmly between his hands so that Eoin could not move his head.

For a mere second Harry thought he felt a presence behind him. He hardly felt the knife at his throat so swiftly did it take place, but he was conscious of life draining from him. Having done what they had committed themselves to do, the men silently left the bathroom. Moments later, without Eoin having a chance to see what had happened, the teenaged boys and Eoin walked out into the station. Only when they were outside the restroom did the young man release his hands from Eoin's head.

"Take your clothes," the teenager said as he handed Eoin a paper bag with his school uniformed rolled up inside. "Walk until the count of twenty, and then throw the tunic in the trash and put on your blazer and cap. Continue until you come upon a policeman. Tell him your name, and he will do the rest to get you home."

"Harry hasn't come out yet. I must wait for Harry."

"Harry is in good hands and he wants you to follow our instructions," one of the young men said while the other removed the 'out of order' sign from the door of the men's room.

The boy did as he was told. After taking a few steps, however, he turned around, but the teenagers were nowhere to be seen.

Harry Browne was dead on arrival at the hospital.

Francis Egan had given notice at his place of employment when the kidnapping first made the headlines. He went to the police station when Eoin was found and requested they release the child to him. He gave assurances he would return Eoin to his mother in Ireland. They consented.

Francis, on a cold autumn day in mid-November, sailed from Wales to Dublin. At this their first meeting, Francis introduced himself to Eoin; whereby, Eoin told Francis he already knew him.

"You do? I don't believe we've met before."

Eoin told Francis of the wedding picture his mother had once kept in the top drawer in the kitchen of the cottage. She had told him he could take it out and look at it at any time, and it was now on the desk in their living room in Dalkey.

Francis smiled. His world was complete. Yes, they had a few hurdles to clear, but he was going home after a long self-imposed exile, and he was given the honor of escorting young Eoin, a delightful boy, home. Francis felt happier at this moment than he felt since he left Ireland.

"I want to see my Mom."

"So do I."

In the course of their conversation, Eoin said, "Harry wasn't nice to Maude."

"Who is Maude?"

"She's the woman who was with us in the flat. She went out to buy the fish and chips. She was nice, but Harry was always mean to her. She called me 'ducks' and 'duckie.' She bought chocolate for me and cigarettes for herself with the change she received when Harry sent her out for food."

"It sounds like you had a friend in Maude."

"Where will Maude go now that Harry's dead?"

"I don't know, Eoin. Back to her family, I suppose."

"Maybe we should go back and bring her with us to Ireland!"

"I believe your mother has a house full of people as it is. Besides, England is Maude's country. She probably wouldn't want to leave it. We all want to be home in our own countries."

"I want to be home with my own mom."

"That's understandable. Home is where those we love live."

"Where do you live?" Eoin asked.

Francis was momentarily left speechless. "Well, at the moment I'm not sure."

"I thought married people lived in the same house. Why do you not live in Mom's house?"

When Francis hesitated in his reply, the boy continued. "Do you not like us?"

"I love you both very much."

This confused Eoin. This man who was his father had said 'home was where the people we loved lived,' but he does not live with us. Not able to decipher what his father meant, Eoin decided to wait until he saw his mother. He could ask her.

Eoin enjoyed being up on deck where he could see the full sweep of the Irish Sea and only left the boat rail when Francis suggested they go the dining room to eat. By then, the boy was shivering from the cold. Francis pulled out an Aran sweater from his duffle bag and wrapped it around his son. Eoin, who was ravenous, did not speak again until he had eaten a good portion of all the food on his plate.

"Maude said Harry was my father, but Harry said that was a lie when we were in the bathroom at the train station." Eoin, in his belief that adults had the all the answers, hoped Francis might clarify all this for him.

"Harry was someone your mother knew before she and I met."

"But Mom married you?"

"Yes. Peoples' lives are not like math where two and two always make four. Instead, they are emotional entities which at times don't seem to make sense. Harry wasn't a good person, and he caused your mom a lot of heartache, but in the end, he showed great bravery."

"If he didn't come and find me in the toilets, might these men have killed me?"

"I wouldn't think so."

"Why did Harry kidnap me?"

"To hurt your mother by taking you from her."

"Did he hate her?"

"Love and hate are opposite ends of the spectrum, but sometimes they join forces. I believe Harry loved your mother and also hated her, due to his own inadequacy and the fact that she refused to let him ruin her life. She had fought back and won. This time she nearly lost, but Harry managed one heroic deed, which is what enables us to be going home today."

"Did you not like Harry?"

"I didn't know him very well."

As the boat came into Dun Laoghaire harbor, Eoin and Francis saw a lot of familiar faces: Kate, Mr. O'Toole, Genevieve, and about a dozen old neighbors from the lane. There were some people whom Francis had not met: Rory and Gwen, Eoin's school companions, neighbors from their new community, all of whom had kept watch with Kate. Eoin, getting off the boat, ran to his mother. Kate, who tried very hard not to cry, did just that on embracing her son. There were tears of joy mixed with tears of horror at what might have happened, and nearly did happen to him. Kate did not seem able to let go of the boy.

"He's safe now, Kate. You can release the boy," O'Toole said gently separating mother and son after some time had elapsed. "There is someone else here who could use a welcoming home from you," and O'Toole stepped aside so that Francis was standing in front of her.

Each of them had visualized this moment and what they would say, but now they hesitated, each uncertain of the other. Breaking the impasse, Francis held out his arms and Kate eased into his embrace, and they were transported back to an earlier, more innocent time when Kate had said, "Yes, I will marry you."

"I'm sorry, Kate, truly sorry. After I left, and I got over my hurt feelings, and my anger subsided, I became embarrassed by my behavior towards you. I didn't know if you'd want me back after my dreadful behavior. I thought I might redeem myself if I worked hard and saved so we could afford the things we wouldn't have been able to have if I'd stayed in Dublin. I thought, like Eoin O'Toole, that I, too, would come back a wealthy man. Of course, O'Toole having become wealthy while working overseas was probably just a rumor. Why else would he live in a small cottage in the lane? Although I was earning a better wage in London, the cost of living there was higher. When I left the bookstore to work on a farm, I did manage to save a respectable sum, but Aunt Mary then told me you had come into an inheritance, making my savings inconsequential. I discovered the longer I stayed away, the more difficult it was to return. A year might have been forgivable, but three years or more absence was a lot less forgivable. Things didn't work out as I thought they would. I was just burying myself in a hole."

"Let's just forgive each other and bury the pain in that hole rather than you."

Francis smiled, "It's done."

"I put the government's compensation money for the cottage in a bank for you."

"The cottage became yours when I left. That money is yours."

"No, it's yours."

"All right, it's ours," Francis laughed, as did Kate.

"Am I going to get an introduction?" Rory, seeing Kate and Francis laugh together after what had seemed like a very serious conversation, came forward and inquired.

"My brother, Rory, and this, Rory is . . ." she was about to say her husband but the word wouldn't come out, "Francis."

"Well, nice to finally meet my brother-in-law," Rory said, firmly grasping Francis' hand. "And this, Francis, is my wife Gwen," he added, as Gwen joined them and poked her husband in the back to let him know of her presence.

Brother-in-law! He accepts me into the family. What a nice fellow. What do they know of our break-up?

"That's Momma over there," Kate broke into his inner conversation.

O'Toole went to speak with the media who were impatiently waiting behind the police barricade, and then the photographers came forward and took pictures.

After the lane people hugged Eoin and Francis, telling them how happy they were to see them both home safe and sound, they loaded Eoin down with chocolates. These good friends refused Kate's invitation to come back to the house, wishing instead to give Kate, her son, and husband this precious time to be alone together to rediscover their relationships.

"Francis and Eoin must be hungry after their trip, and you, Kate, haven't eaten a decent meal during all this upheaval. So, may I suggest Gwen and I take the seven of us out for dinner?"

"A gallant suggestion, Rory," O'Toole, who had just joined in, said. Genevieve, who stood beside him, agreed.

Kate, seated between her husband and son, turned to the boy and said, "I'm sure you have many questions to ask about all that has happened."

"Not really. I already asked your husband a lot of things."

"My husband," Kate softly spoke so none other than Eoin could hear. "I believe, young man, you will need to refer to him as your father now that he is back and living with us. What do you think?"

"I like him," the boy answered with a wide smile, and Kate hugged him.

"If you two need time to get reacquainted, Francis, you can bunk down temporarily in my room," O'Toole said later in the night when they were out of hearing range of the others.

"Thanks, I'll take you up on that if I don't get a better offer," the younger man replied with a smile.

"Eoin is very attached to O'Toole," Francis observed.

"Yes, Francis, old Eoin has been very good to both of us."

"O'Toole was a curiosity factor in the lane, because he never spoke to anyone. People of my parents' age knew that, when growing up, he lived with his parents and brother in one of the big houses on the main road and that he went abroad for several years before returning and moving into a cottage in the lane. It was rumored he displeased his parents, and they cut him off from any inheritance. Nobody knew for sure what happened between him and his father to cause him to take up residence in the lane. He didn't speak with anyone, so how did Eoin and you get to know him?"

"He came down with pneumonia one winter when Eoin was a baby. I attended him."

"Well, I didn't really know him, but on All Hallows', as far back as I can remember, there was always a pound note attached to the sweets he put into my bag," Francis told her. "As I grew older, the pound note became a five-pound note, then a ten-pound note, and on my last year to go trick-or-treating, when I was thirteen years old, a twenty-pound note was inconspicuously attached to the chocolate. That was a huge amount of money at the time. Nobody else among my friends received money. I told my mother when I received the first of these gifts. She asked that I tell no one. It would be our secret. I did as she instructed. I've always wondered why he chose me as the recipient of his gift. My encounter with him as a child was but a few seconds once a year."

"He has done likewise for Eoin," Kate revealed, "and, just as when you were a child, Eoin has been the only recipient of his generosity."

"But you helped O'Toole through his sickness, and he repaid you by his kindness to Eoin. That is reasonable. My parents didn't have any communications with O'Toole. I had no ties to him. So what caused his generosity to me?"

"You'll have to ask him that, Francis."

"Yes, I will, now that this small mystery has become an even bigger one."

CHAPTER 15

Eoin had become a celebrity on his return to school. In order to give Eoin some peace and allow the students to concentrate on their lessons, the master invited Eoin to recall his adventure at assembly the next day.

That evening, his mother and Francis spoke with him and suggested he write it all down on paper in preparation for the task ahead. Francis volunteered to go with him as moral support, although he did not like the limelight and was more nervous than Eoin.

Eoin's friends also told of their involvement and what the Garda had said about their helpfulness in solving the case. In the course of giving their account, the boys mentioned that they had spoken to the Garda two days after Eoin had been kidnapped.

"Two days later!" the master uttered in disbelief. "Why didn't you two go to the Garda immediately?"

The boys did not have a good answer to that question, and after an embarrassing moment of silence, the master gave them time to recoup and took the opportunity to advise the other students that, should they witness anything like this event or anything else that seemed out of order, they should hurry home and phone the Garda immediately. If they did not have a phone at home, they should go the nearest pub where the owner would make the call for them.

"What an orator! Eoin has the makings of a great lawyer," Francis said, as he, Kate, and O'Toole sat around the table at supper that evening.

"What would you like to be when you've grown into manhood?" O'Toole asked.

"A doctor," the boy answered without hesitation.

"Why a doctor?"

"Because I want to make people well just like Mom does."

A hearty round of applause brought delight to the boy.

Mary and Ned phoned and invited them all to the farm for Christmas Eve into Christmas Day. They also extended the invitation to Genevieve, Rory, Kieran, and their families.

"I'm so glad they invited Momma. Now she doesn't have to make the difficult choice of making Christmas dinner for my brothers and their families, or being with us for Christmas. Now we can all be together."

"I'm glad they have invited Genevieve, because I enjoy her company," O'Toole added.

"I wouldn't have thought Momma and you would become such good friends," laughed Kate.

"Aw, for a while it was an uphill journey. I took small steps at first—a walk in the twilight. While walking, she surprised me by thanking me for all the help I had extended to her daughter and grandson during his disappearance. That was, as they say, the beginning of a beautiful friendship. I believed Humphrey Bogart said that in 'Casablanca.' She accepted my invitation of a train ride along the coast with a stop off for a bite to eat and a show I thought she might like to see—a comedy at the Gate Theater. Soon we were both enjoying being in each other's company. I am honored to be able to call Genevieve my good friend."

Mary and Ned led the group into church on Christmas Eve, followed by Kate, young Eoin and Francis, with Genevieve and Eoin in the rear. As they stood for the entrance hymn, Kate inwardly smiled, and her face sparkled bright with joy. This was what she had long waited for and often despaired of happening. She had not been this happy in church at Christmas since her father had stood beside her when she was a child, and with childhood innocence, she believed nothing bad could ever happen to her with him close by. Now, aware that none can protect us from pain or sorrow, she looked over at Francis and knew that together they could handle whatever fate strewed in their path.

As Kate thanked God for Eoin's safe return, she thought of Harry. *Harry had not only not harmed Eoin, he gave his life for him. No matter how much he disliked me and wished to injure me, Harry could not hurt his son. There is good in all of mankind, but only when put to the test, was Harry's goodness revealed.*

My family, Francis thought with pride. *Eoin calls me Dad! Kate loves me. I love her. To love and be loved is all that each of us hopes to achieve. And then there is fate. If Kate had not been wronged by Harry, I would have gone home that night after eating in the pub and never have met Kate. Harry unwittingly brought us together. He did not harm their son, not wholly because Eoin was his son, but because Harry, in his own peculiar way, loved Kate. He forfeited his life for her as much as for the boy. God rest his soul.*

While Francis had gone out to see Ned and Mary two days after his return, Eoin's arrival at the farm was another homecoming for them. "Thank God you were there to take this precious boy home," Mary said after she hugged both Eoin and Francis. "And you, Kate, having to go through that terrible ordeal . . ."

"Mary had every candle in the church burning," Ned interrupted.

"There was nothing else we could do but pray," Mary added. "Now, not only is Eoin home, but Francis has returned to the fold."

"You're making me sound like a lost sheep." This brought laughter to all present.

"When I knew you were coming home, I went looking for a suitable horse for you, but I want you to see her before I seal the deal," Ned told him.

"Did something happen to Roan?"

"No, she's in fine fettle, and waiting for Kate to ride her."

"Roan is your horse, Francis. You must choose which you'd prefer to ride: this other horse or Roan," Kate said.

"We could go over tonight, if you wish," Ned suggested.

"Yes, I'd like to see her, but you know I trust your judgment when it comes to horses."

Ned, Francis, and Eoin O'Toole drove the thirty miles to a

neighboring farm to see the horse. By lantern light they inspected it, and liking what they saw, the horse was purchased and they arrived back at the farm at two o'clock in the morning.

When they got back they found a horse trailer, attached to a BMW, parked in front of the house. Ned and Francis went over to welcome this early morning visitor to the farm, while O'Toole bade them goodnight. They discovered it was Mr. Fitzgerald's stable foreman who, on seeing them get out of the car, introduced himself and explained his reason for being there. Mr. Fitzgerald, who had been following the abduction of the boy, was very pleased, very pleased indeed, to know that the boy was safely brought home by his father. To celebrate this occasion, Mr. Fitzgerald wished to present Eoin Egan with a yearling.

"How long have you been here?" Ned asked.

"About two hours."

"You must have arrived right after we left. Have you left the poor thing locked up in the box?" Ned asked with concern.

"No, sir, since nobody was awake when I got here, I settled it in with hay and water."

"Ah, good man, good man," Ned said, to which the foreman replied, "We take good care of our horses."

"Yes, of course."

"His pedigree is all here," the foreman said, handing Francis a large envelope.

"Let's go see it," Francis said, and they went to the barn and were struck by the beauty and nobility of this fine yearling. After much admiration of this new addition to the farm, Ned spoke.

"What a generous gift. The man you work for must be a very fine man."

"That he is."

Ned insisted the foreman join them for breakfast, and he gladly did. Over a meal of bacon, sausages, eggs, fried pudding, and homemade bread with fresh creamery butter, cooked by Ned and Francis, the conversation throughout breakfast continued to be of horses.

A sleepy Eoin appeared in his pajamas and was told of Mr. Fitzgerald's gift.

"Dad, can I go out and see it?"

Francis, hearing the excited boy call him dad, looked with pride on the lad and answered, "Get your boots and jacket on, and we'll go out."

Moments later, with his arm around the boy's shoulders, they went to the stalls followed by the foreman and Ned who wanted to witness the boy's joy.

"She's a bit skittish. I suggest now that we've all seen her, we leave her to settle in," Francis said.

"That's a good suggestion," the foreman said.

"Please thank Mr. Fitzgerald from Kate, myself, and Eoin for this most generous gift to our son," Francis said as he walked to the car with the foreman, who insisted he must be back at the farm by four in the morning.

On wakening later in the morning, the womenfolk were told of the night's adventure and the wonderful gift from Brian Fitzgerald.

"What a beauty," Kate softly uttered on seeing this small, elegant creature.

Francis conveyed to Kate the foreman's words that Mr.

Fitzgerald welcomes her, Eoin, himself and other family members, at anytime, to drop in at his farm where he personally would be most pleased to show them around.

"This Fitzgerald must be a fine gentleman. Imagine giving the boy such a beautiful animal," Ned addressed O'Toole as they sat by the fire while Mary, Kate, and Genevieve made preparations for the noonday meal. Kate did not previously mention having had dealings with Fitzgerald, and so O'Toole did not bring the matter up. None of Kate's family knew what turmoil she had gone through.

Genevieve noted that Francis and Eoin had been out with the yearling a long time.

"It's difficult to get two good horsemen away from the stables, Ned explained.

"What a delicious aroma coming from the kitchen," O'Toole said as he closed his eyes and breathed in the smell of roasting turkey. Looking at her watch, Genevieve remarked that Francis, Ned and young Eoin should lie down before the rest of the family arrived, as they had been up the greater part of the night.

"Say no more, Genevieve," and rising, O'Toole went to the door and saw that they were on their way in. When they entered, O'Toole stated Genevieve's request, saying, "It's off to bed with you for a few hours until the rest of the family arrive."

"I wish to rest also," and rising, O'Toole headed for the bedroom.

About half past eleven that morning, a car pulled up in front of the house, and young Eoin running and forgetting his manners, called to his uncle Rory, excitedly telling him about the new yearling while completely ignoring his remaining relatives. Kieran and his wife smiled at Eoin's enthusiasm, and as they walked to the house, passed Francis, who wished them a Merry Christmas. Francis then addressed Eoin, "Aren't you going to invite your cousins to see the horse?"

"We're not allowed to go to the barn," Nora told him, "Mommy said we'd get our clothes dirty if we went there."

"Well, let's see this horse, young man, and we'll see you all back at the house," Rory replied, as he, Gwen, and Francis went with Eoin to the stable.

Deirdre was not following her sister to the house, but was trailing behind the group toward the stable.

"Deirdre, you're forbidden to go there. You'll be in a lot of trouble if you do."

Deirdre ignored her sister's warning and quickened her pace until she was part of the advancing group.

When they got to the stable, Eoin, having heard Nora's words to her sister, offered to bring the foal out of the barn so that Deirdre might see it and rub her hand along its warm body without disobeying her mother. But Deirdre walked into the stable and over to where the horse stood.

"It's beautiful," she whispered, as though not to frighten the horse, and timidly placed her hand on its back.

"He is indeed," Gwen agreed.

After much admiration of this new member of the stable, young Eoin asked Deirdre if she would like to see the horse he rode.

"Yes, yes," she answered, and so he brought her over to see it.

"Would you like to sit on her?"

"Yes," the girl answered in contained delight.

"Come over to the side, and I'll help you mount," Francis said. The girl sat on the horse, and uttered with sheer wonder, "Oh, Eoin, you're so lucky to have a horse."

"I could walk her around with you on her, if you wish." All Deirdre could do was smile at the prospect, whereupon, Eoin called to the saddleless horse to follow as he walked out of the stable into the cold sunlit morning.

"I feel like the Queen of Sheba," Deirdre laughed, as she sat upright on the chestnut-color pony as Eoin walked it along a trail out of sight of the house.

As the family sat around the dinner table at the end of the meal, Genevieve said, "I'm so glad the whole family is gathered here together this Christmas, and I'm so very grateful to Mary and Ned for making this all possible." She paused a moment and remained standing. "While we're all together, Eoin and I wish to make an announcement," she said, looking across at the elder Eoin, and added, "Will you take it from here, Eoin?"

"Gladly, my dear. Now that Francis is safely home, it's time I moved out of Kate's and Francis' home, and so Genevieve and I have decided to buy a house that is about a twenty-minute walk from their home."

"Mother," Kieran gasped with alarm.

"Perhaps we should have mentioned that we plan to marry," Genevieve smiled. "We plan a very small wedding with just the immediate family."

"What about your house in Gory?"

"That house, Kieran, I plan to sell."

"Sell the family home!!"

"That house lost its family quite awhile back. You're all married with homes of your own, and I certainly don't want to hold onto that big house."

"Breda, the girls, and I have always joined you for dinner there on Sundays. It was tradition. It is our childhood home!"

"It was in Dublin, Kieran, that we grew up. We were nine and eleven years old when we moved to Wexford. It was Kate who spent her childhood in that house."

"And now the move is back to Dublin to accommodate Kate!"

"Oh, grow up, big brother," Rory responded.

Kieran stood up, threw his napkin down and walked out of the house.

Genevieve felt grieved by this outcome to her and Eoin's plans. Eoin put his arm around her and drew her close to him then spoke. "I thank you, Kate, for your kindness to me in making me feel at home in your home. You and Francis may someday have another child or two and will need the room I am presently using. Young Eoin gave up his room whenever his grandmother came to visit, and we both are grateful to him for that. Now it's time we moved on."

Breda sat silently and listened to all that was said. Kieran returned to the room, but not to the table.

"You didn't even ask me if I would like to buy the house," he addressed his mother. "All these years I took care of your finances, and you did not discuss this with me."

Genevieve did not reply. The room was awash in silence until Kieran again spoke.

"It was our inheritance," he said in a low, angry voice.

On hearing this unfamiliar word again, Eoin announced, "I've got an inheritance."

All looked towards the boy except Eoin O'Toole who tried to make eye connect with Kate, but she, too, was looking at the boy.

"You have?" Rory asked.

"Yes. But I cannot have it until I've grown up."

That was Kate's and my secret, Eoin O'Toole thought.

"Do tell us about it," said Gwen, intrigued by the child's announcement.

"It's from Grandma, and it belonged to Grandpa Eoin, who is dead."

"Oh, how exciting. What is it?"

"It's his pocket watch, and it plays music," he told Gwen.

"You gave him father's watch? I'm the eldest. That should have been mine."

The boy was confused. His uncle has just stated that his inheritance, which his mother was keeping for him, was not his but his uncle's.

Francis, seeing his son's confusion, said, "Come Eoin, and let's walk off some of this fine meal we've had."

The boy gladly arose from the table and followed Francis. Ned joined them. Deirdre stood up and was about to follow when her father asked where she was going. When she said she, too, was going outside, Kieran raising his voice, told her to sit down.

Kate gathered the dishes, brought them to the sink, removed any remaining food from the dishes, and put them in the sink while Mary, seeing Kate's action, picked the pot of boiling water off the stove and poured it into the sink.

"We'll need some cold water to add to this boiling water," she addressed Rory, while holding out a large jug. He immediately took the jug and went out to the rain barrel to fill it.

"You can help wipe the dishes, if you wish," Kate said looking at Deirdre. The girl was glad to be excused from the table. Kate handed her a dishcloth while she removed the remaining food from the table and washed the wooden table down, something she would not have normally done while people still sat at the table.

"I think it is time we went home," Kieran said to his wife, and she and Nora stood up.

Deirdre stopped drying the dishes and stood, not knowing what to do.

"You had better get your gifts and your coat, and go, too. Thank you for helping with the dishes," Kate smiled at her niece and bent over and kissed her.

Having collected all their belongings, Kieran and his family got into their car and left. Deirdre waved to Eoin, and he to her, as the car pulled out into the road.

On a cold, blustery, yet sunny Saturday morning in March, Eoin and Genevieve exchanged vows. Kieran and his family did not return for his mother's wedding, sending their regrets due to their daughter Deirdre's illness. Eoin's brother, accompanied by his wife and their son and daughter-in-law, attended the wedding to Eoin's delight. Rory and his wife, Ned and Mary, young Eoin, and Kate and Francis were also there. A breakfast was served in Francis and Kate's home after a nuptial mass.

Eoin hugged his brother at the luncheon and said, "So glad, Dermot, that you have come to the prodigal son's wedding."

"The prodigal son has gotten himself a grand family, yes, a grand family indeed. And the young boy is your namesake?"

"Well, his grandfather, Genevieve's deceased husband, Eoin, is the person for whom the boy was named. He's a fine young man, and I'm glad to claim him as a grandson."

"How did you manage to talk that lovely lady into marrying you?"

"I proposed with the possibility of being turned down, and instead my proposal was accepted."

Both men laughed and were soon joined by the others. After the wedding breakfast at the Egan's, Genevieve and Eoin invited the guests over for a drink and to show them their new home. Since most of the work they were having done on the house was almost completed, they decided to spend their marriage night there before leaving the following morning for Majorca where they would spend a week.

Rory and Gwen, Francis and Kate, and Eoin went to the airport to see the newlyweds off, as did Dermot, his wife, son, and daughter-in-law on this, the beginning of a new life for them.

CHAPTER 16

About six months after the O'Tooles returned from Majorca, Francis and Kate raised the doorknocker on the older couple's door shortly after nine o'clock on a rainy April evening. Kate and Francis smiled at each other as they waited in happy anticipation. Francis bent over and kissed Kate just as Eoin opened the door.

"Come in, the pair of you," O'Toole said with a grin.

"We realize it's rather late for a visit, but we have some news we want to share with both of you," Francis said, as he followed Kate into the house.

"By the look on your faces, I'd say it is good news you have to impart. Here, Kate, let me have your wet umbrella, and I'll put it into the kitchen sink."

Genevieve, hearing their voices, came into hall and hugged each of them.

"Let's not stand here in the hall. Come in and sit down," Genevieve urged.

"I hope you two weren't getting ready for bed," Kate stated.

"Oh no, love, this is a lovely surprise." Then with concern in her voice, and noting the lateness of the hour, asked, "Is everything all right?"

"Better than all right," Francis smiled.

"Eoin was about to make some cocoa when we heard the knock on the door. Would you like some?"

"Don't go palavering on, woman," Eoin advised in a kindly manner, as he sat down beside her. "The children are bursting to tell us some news." Genevieve put her hand on his, and he covered it affectionately with his other hand. Two faces with great expectations looked at the younger couple. Francis looked at Kate and said, "You, Kate, love, tell them."

"We've just come from a visit to the doctor's office. We expecting."

Genevieve was so overcome by this joyful news that tears broke above the smile on her face. Going towards them, she hugged her daughter, then Francis. Eoin followed suit.

"Well, no cocoa tonight. A toast for this grand occasion," Eoin said going to the liquor cabinet. "What will it be for you Genevieve?"

"A little brandy, please."

"And for you Kate?"

"I'll have the same."

"Brandy all around," Eoin said as he began to pour.

"This is a wonderful surprise," Genevieve said, brimming with joy.

"Yes, indeed, the very best," Eoin agreed.

After the expectant parents were toasted, Kate spoke.

"The doctor told us I was carrying twins. We told him he must be mistaken for there weren't any twins on Francis' side of the family, nor mine."

"That is not so," Genevieve said in a quiet voice. "I was a twin."

"But Mother, I thought you were an only child! Who was this twin who was never spoken of and whom Rory, Kieran, nor I ever saw in the family photograph album?"

"Her name was Katherine. We shared the same crib, my mother told me. She said we babbled and laughed constantly with each, happy just being in each other's company. We were inseparable, my mother and mother's sister had said. When my mother came to our room in the morning to get us washed and dressed, she could hear us babble before she opened the door to the bedroom. She had to lift both of us out of the crib together, since taking one of us out of sight of the other, even if only for a short time, left the other twin fretful.

"Mother recalled telling my father one night that she had separated us so that we were now at opposite ends of the crib, because she thought it wasn't healthy for us to sleep tangled together. As my father retired for the night a little later in the evening, he checked in on us. Getting into bed he told my mother we were sleeping like Siamese twins, and he could not tell which arms or legs belonged to Katherine or me."

"What happened to Katherine?"

"She got sick and died soon after." Genevieve paused a moment before continuing. "My parents said I was inconsolable. I stopped babbling and laughing and didn't want to eat. They didn't know what to do for me, and I wouldn't respond to anyone. They got a life-sized baby doll and put it in my crib to comfort me, but I just stared at it. When they brought it closer to me, I reached out and touched the doll like Katherine and I touched. I immediately screamed in horror and fear. Apparently, I had thought it was another baby, and by touching it, felt its cold china hand."

"Why didn't you tell me about your sister?" Kate gently asked.

"We were only ten months old when it happened. All I have of her is what my mother told me. A loss, a forgotten consciousness stored away somewhere. I wanted to call you Katherine. Your father, understandably, did not want his beautiful daughter named after a dead child. Your name is Katherine on your birth certificate, but he insisted you were to be called Kate." Genevieve grew quiet. Kate embraced her mother.

After a moment, Eoin asked, "May I refresh your drink, love?" She shook her head.

"No, love, I'm fine. It's painful even after so many years but also good to be able to speak of this incident long-buried within me." Turning to Kate, Genevieve continued.

"After Katherine was removed from the crib, I apparently went mute, for there was no one to babble with. I lost weight. My parents became alarmed, fearing they might lose their remaining child. They agreed to have me hospitalized. I remained at the hospital for a fortnight. During that time, no matter when my parents came to visit me, I was always in one of the nurse's arms. The nurses sang to me, and they played with me. My mother and father were so happy I was receiving such good care. I was babbling again, not to the degree I had done with my twin, but my smile and any kind of baby noise coming from me was a delight to them. Even if I awoke during the night, one of the nurses picked me up. Soon, I was eating and gaining weight, and preparations were being made for me to leave the hospital.

"When the day arrived for my discharge from the hospital, all the nurses hugged and kissed me goodbye, then handed me to my mother. When she was leaving with me in her arms, I screamed and held out my arms toward the nurses. Mother was distraught by this rejection. When I wouldn't stop crying, she handed me to my father, but I continued to cry pitifully. Father ignored the stares and strange looks he was getting from people who came into or left the hospital. Afterwards, he said he felt like he was kidnapping a child, and was expecting the police to arrive before we left the hospital grounds."

"'The nurses had spoiled my little girl,' Mother had said.

Genevieve sat quietly for a few moments, as though still living in a time past. Eoin sat down beside her and held her hand. Moments later, Genevieve smiled up at him and gave him the courage to speak.

"Now that the past is being shared, I too, have something I need to reveal concerning Francis and myself."

"Perhaps we should have some tea before you do so," Francis offered.

"Tea can wait, son."

It was then, as the four of them sat together, that Eoin revealed to Francis the story of his birth as he had told Kate many years earlier while she nursed him back to health.

After the initial shock wore off, Francis wanted to know why Eoin had waited so long to tell him, since his parents were both long dead, and why he chose this day to reveal it.

"I should have told you a long time ago, yes. At first, I had to wait until you could understand the ways of love, so that our actions would not sully your mother in your eyes. I don't know how you will see it, but I believed and still believe it was an act of pure love on our part. I gave the woman I loved what she wanted most, a child, and she in turn presented her young husband with what he most craved, a child.

"Then it was imperative that I step completely out of the picture. You had two excellent parents. If Aoife's husband had mistreated you in any way, I would have come to your rescue, but the man you knew as your father was one of the best people I've ever known.

"Knowing when to impart this delicate information to you has been the bane of my life. I woefully regretted not making your origin known to you before you left the lane for England. You might have shared your plans to leave Ireland with me, if you had known and accepted me as your father. I could have made known to you at that time my strong belief that if Aoife's husband had discovered who fathered you, he still would have accepted you wholeheartedly and continued to love both of you.

"To answer your second question, I could wait no longer to reveal that I am your father, because two children will arrive in the New Year, and I want to rightly claim them as my grandchildren."

"And you shall," Francis laughed. "You have also solved the mystery of why I always received a generous gift from you on All Hallows."

"Well, I couldn't give you a gift for Christmas, as I would have wished, and so I gave a gift to you on All Hallows when it could be received unnoticed by anyone."

"When I told my mother of this unusual gift, she asked that I let it remain our secret, revealing it to none other. I promised I would. Kate told me you did the same for young Eoin, even though you knew he wasn't my biological son."

"You are my biological son. Kate is your wife, my daughter-in-law and Eoin's mother, and I love all three of you."

"Am I the last person in this room to have received this information?"

"Yes, son, but it was definitely not by plan. When Kate was alone with a young child, she revealed to me her indiscretion. I, in turn, revealed mine. Our two lost souls became kindred spirits.

"Not wanting any secrets between us, I told Genevieve before I asked her to marry me." In the silence that followed, Francis' mind seemed to have wandered beyond the boundaries of the living room.

"Is there something that is troubling you, Francis?"

"If you had died before the man I knew as my father, I would never have known you were my father, and there would be no proof of your ever having had a child."

"Love needs no proof."

Francis stood up and walked towards Eoin and within arms reach of each other, they simultaneously reached out and clasped one another in a long embrace.

"Dad," the young man said, and was answered by the single word, "Son."

Afterwards Genevieve said she would make the tea. Francis said it was late, and they had better go home so as not to keep their neighbor, who was staying with Eoin, up too late.

"Now, all secrets are out in the open," Kate said. Then looking around at all, added, "They are, aren't they?"

"Yes, thank God," Eoin laughed.

"Kate, I'd like you to come to Gory with me, so each of us can take whatever we want from the house before it and its contents are auctioned," Genevieve suggested.

"When?"

"Sunday would be good. Do you have Sunday off, Kate?"

"Yes, I do, and will happily go with you."

"I hope you two gentlemen will help in getting the things we choose to keep into Francis' truck, and bringing them up to Dublin."

"I'm free," Eoin stated.

"As am I," Francis added.

"Then it's all settled for Sunday. We'll all meet here for breakfast after the eight o'clock mass, have breakfast, and leave right after, if that's agreeable to all."

It was.

When they arrived at the house in Gory, Genevieve, horrified by the weeds that had overtaken her usually well-maintained garden, sighed.

"Don't worry, love. Francis and I will do battle with those weeds while you and Kate do your sorting indoors."

"Thank you both," responded the grateful Genevieve.

As she entered the house, Kate asked, "You will miss this house, will you not?"

"Yes and no. I always regretted agreeing to move here from Dublin." Before Kate could ask another question, her mother spoke.

"Let's start upstairs in the storage area and work our way down."

"What storage area?"

"In the master bedroom there is a door that leads into a partially finished room. We did not need another room, and so we used it for storage. It came in very handy for your father and me when you and your brothers were growing up, because we could lock away birthday and Christmas presents there."

"It's locked?"

"Your father was afraid, since it was an unfinished room, that the boys might come upon it and, in fooling around, fall though the widely-separated plank floor and hurt themselves. So he put a lock on it."

Entering the bedroom, Kate looked around. "I don't see another door."

"It's a low door—over there behind that chair," her mother said, pointing toward it. "One needs to bend down to enter, but once inside, one can stand up."

Kate walked ahead of her mother and removed the chair.

"Taped to the hem of the drapes, you'll find the key."

Kate inserted the key and opened the door. Genevieve stretched her arm in, pulled a cord, and a light came on.

"This is a very large storage area," Kate said in surprise. "Oh good grief, there are all my Hallows' Eve's costumes. You kept every one of them," Kate laughed. "They are lovely."

"The year you deemed yourself too grown up to go trick-or-treating, you told me you had hated every one of them."

"It was very cruel of me to say that. They are beautiful. It wasn't the costumes I disliked; it was being different that I objected to. All the other children wore old hand-me-down clothes, or an assortment of things they themselves had put together. The other children would ask if I was going to a fancy dress ball and say things that made me want to hide instead of joining in the fun. In my pretty as a picture outfit, I didn't fit in."

"I'm so sorry, Kate. I didn't know the costumes were received by your friends in such a manner. You certainly did look beautiful in them, but it was all spoiled for you by those remarks."

"The librarian scolded some children who pulled at my Bo Peep outfit and laughed."

"Oh, Helena, yes, she was very fond of you. When I go into the library, she always asks how you're doing. I told her about Eoin and what a smart boy he is. She'll be delighted to hear you are going to have twins."

"I had thought you did not like her because of dad's friendliness towards her."

"Heavens, Kate, I'd have had to eliminate everyone in town if that were so. Your father engaged everyone in conversation. It was not Helena that was at fault. It was the state of our marriage at that time. Your father had time for everyone, it seemed, but me. That is what I resented. You, unfortunately, were born into a family with a deteriorating marriage. Not only that, but shortly after you were born I fell into a horrible state of depression which lasted over a year. That very important year of your life, when we should have bonded, was lost to us.

"I lost a great deal of weight. I looked like a skeleton. The doctor wanted to hospitalize me, but I refused to enter the hospital. I was given a list of highly nourishing food items to eat, but I couldn't get them down. I knew it was up to me to break out of that awful state I was in. After looking at you asleep in your crib, I decided the boys were older and did not need me as much. You would be my reason to fight."

"So, what did you do?"

"I gathered all my favorite foods from childhood onwards and began eating. Soon my favorite foods were no longer my favorite foods, but by then I had gained weight. That summer it seemed as though I put ice cream on everything except my tea, until I felt I never wanted to see or taste another scoop of ice cream. My efforts bore fruit. During the time I was nonfunctional, your father took care of you. When I regained my health, you continued to go to him with all your problems and for all your needs."

"How very sad!"

"Yes, yet good. Although I was deeply saddened that I had lost out, I was grateful that he took such good care of you. You were only a baby; you needed at least one parent to attend to your needs.

"When my strength returned I decided I needed to socialize. Eoin spoke with people daily in his practice. When I suggested that I get a job, he would not consider it. So I joined gatherings, even some I had no interest in, in order to meet people. Soon I knew almost everyone in Gory. Then I began to give parties for every occasion that presented itself. My parties were a big hit. Everyone sought an invitation. After a few years, however, I wearied of them and wished to stop, but found that might be quite difficult because the people expected them. The year I sprained my ankle was a blessing that came with pain. That was the year I could finally excuse myself from giving parties. I was out of the loop."

"But you still gave the annual children's Christmas party long after you stopped giving parties for adults, even after I went to boarding school. You planned them for the third day after my return home so that I could unwind before meeting all my friends at the party. I loved those Christmas parties."

"Did you really? You never said so before."

"You invited all the children in town, even the Gillespie boys whom you did not like."

"I did not dislike them. What I disliked was that they were unsupervised and were friends with my daughter."

"That was not their fault."

"Of course not, but if one of your twins is a girl, and we have this discussion when she is eleven or twelve years old, I have a feeling your response will be a lot different. We protect our daughters."

"No, Momma, that's a fallacy."

"What?"

"When a girl gets pregnant she pays the piper, but the boy is rarely held accountable. If the girl has the audacity to say he was the one to impregnate her, he'll deny it. If the girl persists, she may be accused of having sexual encounters with many men, and so the family name and her name will be thoroughly blackened. So under these circumstances, it is usually deemed a better choice to hide the pregnancy and for her to leave home quietly. She will be sent to a home where she will work until the baby is born, and the child will be put up for adoption."

"Sadly, back then I thought those girls were immoral."

"Did you not question the boy's part in these situations?"

"No. I was part of the kind of thinking you just described. I was thoroughly indoctrinated, as were my peers. You have changed my point of view on these matters. After I got over the hurt that you kept the birth of my first grandson hidden from me (he was four years old before you brought him out of the shadows), I realized, if our roles were reversed, I, too, might not have revealed the birth to someone who thought like me. And so, with much difficulty in finding the lane, I made my way there to apologize."

"I'm very glad you made that trip."

"Are you packing up those Hallows' Eve costumes to discard or to save?"

"To keep," Kate laughed. "Those cribs over there, were they Kieran and Rory's?"

"No, one was mine, and the other was yours."

"I did not know you kept those cribs."

"I did, and your baby carriage, and doll carriage as well."

They both laughed as Kate moved through the boxes and an assortment of objects toward the cribs. Halfway there, she bumped into her roller skates hanging from the rafters. Memories flooded back, lost and forgotten treasures were found, and Kate and Genevieve regaled each other with tales and recollections and much laughter.

"All right, where are you ladies hiding?" Eoin's voice from downstairs rang out loud and clear.

"Come up here," Genevieve answered.

Eoin and Francis ascended the stairs.

"It has taken us more time than we thought," Kate told Francis.

"Your mean you haven't even sorted through the downstairs yet?" Eoin asked in disbelief.

"No, but what we're taking from the storage space in here," Genevieve said, as she pointed to the small open door, "will, no doubt, fill most of the van. So we'll need to plan a second trip."

"That little space?" Francis asked, as he looked towards the low door.

"Go over and look in," Kate urged him. "It's a small door, but it leads to a large room."

"That it does," Francis admitted as he moved out of the way so that Eoin, too, could look into the room.

While Eoin and Francis loaded the van, Kate and Genevieve placed the large cardboard boxes they had brought with them on the floor of the dining room and removed the stacks of newspaper from the boxes. Together they wrapped the Waterford crystal and the china dinner and tea sets in newspaper. In between the layers of crystal and china, they placed bath towels. Soon the van was filled with two cribs, a baby carriage, a child's chest of drawers, toys, games, lamps, a child's desk, an assortment of household objects, and the large boxes Kate and Genevieve had packed.

In the van on the drive home, Eoin spoke.

"What were you ladies doing? You had a whole house full of items to decide upon, and you got no further than a storage room?"

"Sometimes one arrives at a precise moment for good clear conversation, and one must take these moments before they are lost." Genevieve explained.

Eoin shook his head in disbelief.

"Yes," Francis agreed with her. "That's exactly what happened last night when Kate and I arrived at your home to tell you you were going to be grandparents again."

"You're a very insightful young man, Francis," Genevieve smiled.

"There was I under the misconception that last night we had a lifetime of 'precise' moments, all beautifully fulfilled," Eoin responded.

"All right, Momma and I promise to have no more such moments until all the work is done," Kate laughed.

"Eoin and Francis, thank you. You both did a wonderful job weeding, trimming hedges and bushes, and mowing that horribly neglected lawn," Genevieve said as she leaned over and kissed Eoin, then Francis. "That badly neglected house now looks cared for."

Plans had been underway for quite some time when the women from the lane and some neighbors of Kate's from Dalkey arrived at Genevieve's home for a surprise baby shower. Kate, at eight months pregnant with twins, arrived at her mother's home as requested with Francis and their son to see the baby carriage, designed for twins, that her mother and Eoin had purchased for them.

Kate was most pleasantly surprised on entering the house to find a baby shower for her was taking place. Among her mother and so many friends were Mary and Ned. As Kate was drawn into the group, Ned, Eoin, Francis, and young Eoin left the house and walked to the local pub.

Kate and many of her friends from the lane continued to meet once a year for a full day's outing to catch up on the news of their lives. Now at Genevieve's home they all uttered their amazement at the changes in Eoin O'Toole since his days of dwelling in the lane.

"See what a good woman can do for a man," Tara said, to the laughter of all present.

Baby gifts were opened with admiration for the giver and the gift, and baby stories were exchanged between the younger and the somewhat older women, while Kate thanked and hugged and was hugged in return amid much laughter and joy.

After fond remembrance over refreshments, Liz confessed, "In spite of all my present conveniences, I miss the lane and all its people."

"Me, too," Siobhan added.

"For myself, I'd rather be living in the lane," Kathleen added her voice to the lament, "But for my children and grandchildren, I'm glad we're living in a flat with indoor plumbing. My grandchildren can't visualize a home without a bathroom."

"Spoiled is what they are now," laughed Monica.

"Maybe so, but we all want something better for our children," Peg said in a dreamlike fashion.

"I'd like my present living accommodations with all its conveniences to be in the lane," Tara concluded.

"Yes, I suppose that is what all of us want," Kate agreed, "the best of worlds, all the amenities and conveniences in our little village within a village."

CHAPTER 17

Less than a month later, Kate gave birth to twin girls. To the distress of all and the utter devastation of Francis, Kate died just hours after the birth. Francis' grief for his wife was compounded by guilt for the years lost to them by his living in England. That unnecessary absence tortured him.

"Why," in distress, he asked his father, "could Kate give birth to Eoin without any medical assistance in his cottage with no conveniences, and now in a maternity hospital under the watchful eyes of a doctor and nurses, die in childbirth?"

"There is no answer," Francis. "It was by all accounts a more difficult birth than her previous one."

Francis was inconsolable. Anger from his own actions seeped into his grief like oil in water, leaving a terrible residue.

"Kate was like a daughter to me, Francis," his father softly said, as he remembered her first visit to his cottage to nurse him back to health and their conversations. "She reminded me of your mother. I felt honored to be able to help her with her legal entanglement caused by Harry Brown. Although I never met that man, I know him to be evil. How else could he have put Kate through such anguish?"

"Dad, my actions were no better than Harry's. I abandoned

her when she was pregnant. I wasn't there to defend her against Harry's threat. You were more a father to the boy than I was."

"Your reasons were completely different. Harry wanted the boy to please his wife and appease his father-in-law."

"I believe, when Harry got to know young Eoin, he liked the boy. Perhaps he was sorry he wasn't part of the boy's life. Harry saved Eoin's life—partially for Eoin's sake, but mostly because he loved Kate. He, too, had made a mess of his life and lived to regret it before he died."

"Kate forgave your absence from her and Eoin's life. You and Kate were very happy together since your return. Cherish those moment of your life, not only for your sake, but for Eoin and your infant daughters. They are all depending on you. You need to come to terms with Kate's death, for the children's sake."

"You could not marry the woman you loved, nor could you claim your son. I don't have that kind of strength, Dad."

"Yes, you do. You are the product of two people who dearly loved you and the kindness and love of the person you called father."

Eoin bearing his own loss knew he had to be strong in order to help Genevieve through the loss of her only daughter. He helped young Eoin who was so happy that his father returned home and then lost his beloved mother a year later. It was a bittersweet year for the young lad.

In 1961, when John Kennedy was the president of the United States, Kate's cousin, Sheila, returned to Ireland, married, and settled down. Genevieve had hoped the new granddaughters would have been named Katherine and Genevieve for her and her sister, but understood it was Kate's wish, should the babies be both girls, that they be name Aoife and Genevieve to honor both mothers.

Ireland now saw herself in a new light. A new era had begun. To America, who had taken in all who arrived on her shores, Ireland had given an illustrious son. Hope spread across the land.

Kate's funeral took place in Dalkey. Francis drove Ned and Mary in for this sad occasion. They would spend the night with Genevieve and Eoin rather than make the long trip home. Eoin O'Toole, on seeing his reddish-blonde-haired granddaughters, could not help but be reminded of Aoife of long ago. So, too, was his brother Dermot, who came with his wife, their son and daughter-in-law to console the family in their loss and to quietly celebrate the birth of Aoife and Genevieve.

Rory turned to Gwen and remarked on this duel event. "Here we are dressed in black in mourning for Kate, while bearing brightly wrapped gifts for her infant daughters."

Coming towards Gwen and Rory, Eoin O'Toole asked, "Do you wish to go into the other room to say goodbye to Kate?"

"No," answered Rory, "I wish to always remember Kate, fully alive, as she galloped along the strand in the early morning hours on her beloved horse."

Eoin nodded in acknowledgement of Rory's decision. Gwen agreed.

"From the beginning to the end of life, joyfulness and sadness intermingle," Gwen softly spoke as she tightened her grip on Rory.

"Kate's daughters will come to know their mother and what an exceptional person she was from what they hear of her from the family."

Kieran sat in a corner of the room with head bent down weeping while his wife, unable to console him, stood silently next to him.

Nora and Deirdre begged to hold their redheaded cousins, while Nora lamented how she wished they lived closer to the twins so that they might babysit the girls. Alas, Eoin and Genevieve had already volunteered for this service and would hire a nurse for six months until the twins slept through the night.

Six couples from the lane attended the funeral, plus two women and a boy. He was the Donavan boy who had been Kate's first patient in the lane, and who was now nineteen years old. In a somber day following the funeral, the twins would be baptized.

To the surprise of all, Brian Fitzgerald, who now had a granddaughter of his own, made a brief appearance after the baptism, and was warmly welcomed. Brian told Francis that his long time horse trainer was about to retire, and he offered the position with all of its lucrative benefits to Francis. This was the once-in-a-lifetime opportunity Francis craved, but it came at the worst possible time. He had, therefore, to refuse for many reasons: his life was in turmoil, his beloved wife had died, he had a home in Dalkey, and he would, need to uproot his family or have a long ride to work and back, should he accept Fitzgerald's offer. Eoin would have to change schools and bid his friends goodbye which would add to the already drastic changes in the young boy's life. Genevieve and

Eoin had bought a house within walking distance in order to be close to his family, and he and his children needed them to be close by. There was also Ned and Mary to consider. He had already spent too much time away from his aunt and uncle, and they were no longer able to give the land and animals the care they once did. He knew he would never make a decent salary from the farm and would always remain financially strapped. Yet his was a childhood of wonderful memories, being on the farm during the summer holidays from school, Christmastime, his birthday and other special occasions. As a single man he was contented working along side his uncle.

It was a good life. He had his own cottage, and his aunt, an excellent cook, made meals for all three of them from that which grew on the farm: potatoes, vegetables, and fruit for pies and jam. They raised chicken and pigs, and their cows gave them fresh milk daily. The little cash he received met his needs. Now, however, he must provide for his young family, make mortgage payments and pay other expenses. More importantly, the farm was not the kind of work he wanted and so became like an albatross around his neck.

His uncle, in turning the farm over to Francis, told him he could run it anyway he wanted; he could modernize the milking machinery, for example. It was their fervent wish that he would keep the farm in the family. Francis, however, did not want the farm. He wanted nothing to do with cows, hogs, chickens, or any kind of farm animals. Unlike his uncle, who had always kept a horse for working the fields and driving the cart into town, and a horse for Francis to ride, Francis' sole interest was in horses. He wanted to ride and train horses. Fitzgerald's offer was the kind of opportunity he had always hoped for. Francis wanted desperately to accept Fitzgerald's offer, and it tore at his very soul to have to turn it down. Loss of his beloved Kate combined with the loss of a position he craved but could not accept. Combined with his guilt over the years he spent away from Kate and Eoin, Francis was wrenched at the inner core of his being. *I had everything in life I wanted, and then Kate died.*

His mother would have said 'he was a rich man having three delightful children and poor only in lacking riches.' Kate would have agreed with his mother's statement, he felt. Kate raised their son alone in his small cottage without heat or electricity or money. Kate's happiness came, not through wealth, but through her family and friends.

I must not let Kate down. I cannot let Kate down. I will be here for our children.

Young Eoin introduced Mr. Fitzgerald to his baby sisters and to his school friends. Mr. Fitzgerald had not only given the babies gifts but also, to Eoin's great surprise, gave him a gift, too.

"Take good care of your little sisters, Eoin."

"Yes, sir."

"Not only now when they're young but when they reach their teen years."

"Isn't that what his father is supposed to do?" Niall asked.

Fitzgerald smiled at the boy, then turning back to Eoin, continued. "A parent cannot go where teenagers go. Develop good communications with those two young ladies so that when something is bothering them, they will, in confidence, turn to you."

"Yes, sir."

Brian Fitzgerald put his hand on the boy's shoulder.

"You are young now, but the years go spinning by, and when this advice is needed, I hope you'll make good use of it."

"Yes, sir." Fitzgerald shook hands with the boy.

"See you all at the Dublin Horse Show in August," Fitzgerald said as he reluctantly bid the family goodbye. Walking to his car, Brian Fitzgerald remembered the first time he met Kate who, on seeking her son, found him mounted on one of his horses. On meeting Kate, it was beyond his understanding how Harry Brown could forsake this intelligent, graceful, and most attractive young woman and treat her so shamefully. He was glad his daughter did not bear a child of Harry's. Now Kit was married to the overseer of his farm, a man who cherished his daughter, and together gave him a granddaughter. He wished Kate's life had turned out well. He was greatly troubled by her death. He liked Francis, knew his love for and experiences with horses, and would be happy to have him in his employ.

Aoife and Genevieve had been born the year President Kennedy entered the White House. What had been impossible now seemed possible! It was in this atmosphere, that it was thought, Ireland could be reunited. It was a huge expense for the British government to maintain a presence in Northern Ireland, but they couldn't withdraw without consequences. Those running for political office in England needed Northern Ireland's vote to win an election.

A small group of Irish people began walking in a Gandhi-like demonstration, but they were abused and beaten while the police in Northern Ireland stood by and watched. These demonstrators were idealistic. Soon both sides were involved in reckless killings. The longer the fighting went on, the more bitter and more revengeful each side became, and the harder it was to stop. As the years went by, another generation, who had seen the mistreatment of their people, were enlisted by the IRA, and a terrible era was born.

After Prime Minister Margaret Thatcher stepped down, Tony Blair took office. He did the unexpected; he apologized to the Irish people for England's past atrocity to Ireland. That was the turning point. It helped many people let go of the past. Peace did not happen immediately, but concessions were offered, many rejected and some accepted. It took a long time for peace to take hold.

The standard of living on this small island gradually got better. Emigration was no long deemed a necessity. By the year 1990, Ireland's economy grew and strengthened. It was known as the Celtic Tiger. Many who had left Ireland in earlier years had returned and prospered. In the year 2000, it was said, Ireland had the strongest economy in Europe. It was hoped that the Egan children would grow into adulthood in this new found prosperity. Life, however, with its ever changing capacity, shook this island nation when the European economy collapsed. After its full and plenty years, the Irish economy came crashing to a halt. Loss of jobs, a huge national debt, the declining housing market: this was the new reality. Non-Irish people who had come to work in Ireland at the height of its boom packed up and left.

Francis, who saw Eoin looking at his and Kate's wedding photograph, excused himself from a group of people and walked over to put his arm around the boy. At that moment, Eoin buried his head in Francis' abdomen and cried. After several minutes, the boy withdrew from his father ever so slightly, and wiping his eyes with the back of his hand, asked, "Dad, why did I have three grandfathers?"

"Three?"

"Yes, your father and mother died before I was born as did Mom's father. Yet Grandpa O'Toole is your father. How can that be?"

"Yes, it is a bit complicated. I did not discover Grandpa O'Toole was my father until I returned from England."

"How come you didn't know he was your father?"

"When you are old enough, I will explain it to you as it was explained to me."

"Do I have to be over thirty before it's explained to me?"

"No, son, when you are eighteen and legally a man, I will explain all."

"Is it something, bad—well, not good?"

"Oh, no. It's a wonderful love story which you will better understand when you're more mature." A silence followed wherein the boy's thoughts jumped around in his head. This father thing was very confusing. He had yet another questions to ask.

"Why did Mr. Brown say he was my father when he was not?"

"That, too, will have to wait until you are older."

"Is that a bad story?" The boy thought it surely must be a bad tale.

"No, Eoin. It, too, is a love story but of a different kind." Seeing the confusion on the boy's face, he added, "Love, while it is a wonderful thing, it often produces misunderstandings, and it can also play havoc in our lives."

The boy looked at his father perplexed and with great love.

ACKNOWLEDGEMENTS

My thanks to Aine O'Brien Paulus. She did research and organized a contingent of friends in Ireland: Joyce, The Foleys, and also Tom and Celine Devoy who travelled around Dublin photographing cottages that are the inspiration for the cover.

I also wish to thank The 12 o'clock Scholar's Writing Group, especially Jack Chalfin, Arthur Clarke, Valerie Lane, Ted Richards and all the group for their belief and encouragement in my writing.

AUTHOR

Maura Rooney Hitzenbühler was born in New York, the fourth of seven children of Irish immigrants. When her mother died in childbirth, Maura, only four years old, and her brothers were sent to relatives in Ireland and England, never to live as a family again. *The Lane* is based on her memory of the forgotten places and insular society of Dublin in the Fifties.

On returning to America, Maura became a writer and traveled extensively through Asia, Latin America, Europe and the Middle East. A frequent visitor to Ireland, Maura lives and writes on Cape Cod.

Breinigsville, PA USA
18 December 2010

251742BV00002B/2/P